"I've got you. Just anchor yourself to my waist and take slow, deep breaths."

Ed's face was so close to hers she had nowhere to look but into his eyes, his mouth issuing instructions she was compelled to follow.

Georgiana wrapped her arms around his neck, her leg around his middle, which she wouldn't have done in any other circumstances save for the immediate threat of drowning.

She was relying on him saving her, letting him feel her disability for hi‌... he was calming her, taking h‌... that frightened ‌... and syncing his ‌... in and out. Until ‌... left entwined, her ‌... breaths mingling, ‌... moved on from a potential d‌...ing incident to…well, she didn't know what.

Eventually Ed spoke, his voice hoarse as though he was the one who'd inhaled half of the pool. "Are you okay?"

She wanted to say no, she wasn't okay with any of this. Either proving him right that she couldn't be left alone in here or about this overwhelming urge to kiss him.

Dear Reader,

It's been a strange and difficult year for all of us, but I hope I can take your mind off everything for a little while.

Ed and Georgiana live in a kingdom where the pandemic doesn't exist. My hero and heroine are brave, strong and compassionate. Everything we need to be for the foreseeable future.

So strap yourself in for another roller-coaster ride of romance and heartache with my surgeon and my princess. Enjoy!

Karin xx

THE SURGEON AND THE PRINCESS

KARIN BAINE

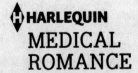

HARLEQUIN
MEDICAL
ROMANCE

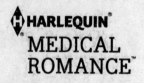

HARLEQUIN®
MEDICAL
ROMANCE™

Recycling programs
for this product may
not exist in your area.

ISBN-13: 978-1-335-40444-2

The Surgeon and the Princess

Copyright © 2021 by Karin Baine

All rights reserved. No part of this book may be used or reproduced in
any manner whatsoever without written permission except in the case of
brief quotations embodied in critical articles and reviews.

This is a work of fiction. Names, characters, places and incidents
are either the product of the author's imagination or are used fictitiously.
Any resemblance to actual persons, living or dead, businesses,
companies, events or locales is entirely coincidental.

This edition published by arrangement with Harlequin Books S.A.

For questions and comments about the quality of this book,
please contact us at CustomerService@Harlequin.com.

Harlequin Enterprises ULC
22 Adelaide St. West, 40th Floor
Toronto, Ontario M5H 4E3, Canada
www.Harlequin.com

Printed in U.S.A.

Karin Baine lives in Northern Ireland with her husband, two sons and her out-of-control notebook collection. Her mother's and her grandmother's vast collection of books inspired her love of reading and her dream of becoming a Harlequin author. Now she can tell people she has a *proper* job! You can follow Karin on Twitter, @karinbaine1, or visit her website for the latest news—karinbaine.com.

Books by Karin Baine

Harlequin Medical Romance

Pups that Make Miracles
Their One-Night Christmas Gift

Single Dad Docs
The Single Dad's Proposal

Paddington Children's Hospital
Falling for the Foster Mom

Reforming the Playboy
Their Mistletoe Baby
From Fling to Wedding Ring
Midwife Under the Mistletoe
Their One-Night Twin Surprise
Healed by Their Unexpected Family
Reunion with His Surgeon Princess
One Night with Her Italian Doc

Visit the Author Profile page
at Harlequin.com for more titles.

With love for my lovely editor, Charlotte,
who is worth her weight in gold! xx

CHAPTER ONE

'ROBO-PRINCESS. PART MACHINE, part fairy-tale heroine.'

Georgiana could almost hear her squad now, as they'd sat joking around her hospital bed after her amputation. It had been their way of trying to cheer her up. The army way, with dark humour disguising their concern and love for one of their own.

She missed her team and the close relationships she'd forged. Since her op, she hadn't had a chance to catch up with them again. More from a sense of shame than lack of opportunity. She didn't want them to pity the person she'd become.

Back then Georgiana had laughed along with the teasing, convinced it was only a matter of time before she'd be back with the others in some capacity as their medic. Now the nickname felt more like a cruel joke. She was neither warrior nor princess. Simply a one-legged failure at both.

There was no way she could go back to the army now, when it was taking all her strength just to live her life unassisted. As for the princess bit—well, she'd never seriously considered that as a career. More of a curse bestowed upon her at birth, being next in line to the throne of Bardot, a small kingdom sandwiched between Liechtenstein and Switzerland that the rest of the world neither knew nor cared about.

The sound of her much-missed squaddies in her head was replaced with the steady thud of her pounding the treadmill. A reminder she was almost back on her feet, even if only one of them was real. At least they were both moving in sync now, so she was no longer walking like an inebriated penguin. Balance was a tricky thing to achieve with only one leg. One and a half if she counted the remaining scarred stump.

She watched herself in the full-length mirror of her home gym. The wounds on her face had faded but she still saw them there, ugly and gaping, like the ones all over her body. Reminders of what she'd gone through and lost.

The explosion rang deafeningly in her ears

once more. The safe walls around her were blown away, replaced with clouds of dust and debris, and she was back there. Clawing the dirt out of her mouth and eyes. Trying to stand and falling. Then she was screaming, 'Medic down!' while tying a tourniquet around what was left of her leg, injecting herself with morphine and waiting as her team leader called a Medevac to fly her to hospital.

Georgiana increased her pace, closed her eyes and tried to outrun the past. It didn't work. Nothing did. Even coming back to Bardot, separating herself from that army environment she'd been encompassed in during rehabilitation, hadn't lessened the pain of what had happened and what it meant for her future. Especially knowing if she'd simply accepted her position here instead of trying to distance herself from the toxicity of the establishment, she'd have remained in one piece.

These were the thoughts she failed to block out day by day in her recovery. Neither the increased heavy pounding of her body on the treadmill nor her laboured breathing could drown them out.

She grabbed the headphones hanging over the handrail and somehow managed to wrestle them on without missing a step. Those tiny, wireless buds were all the rage these days but her old-fashioned padded ones blocked out more of the world. So she was cocooned, safe, surrounded by the familiar music blasting in her ears. It helped her push through the pain barrier, both physically and mentally. If she was to get back any resemblance of her old life she had to keep going. No matter how much it hurt.

Unfortunately, her damaged body couldn't quite live up to the promises she'd made to herself. This was her new normal and she hated the powerlessness over her physical self. She wasn't a quitter, she'd proved that to progress as far as she had in military life. There had been no exceptions made for her, no special favours called in, she hadn't wanted that. She'd worked as hard as any other recruit. Sometimes harder, to prove that she wasn't simply a pampered princess. Well, she had been until she'd made a stand against the life she'd been born into. Swapping it for something more fulfilling.

Now that she'd been forced to leave that much-wanted military life she was lost again. With no true direction or sense of self when everything had been taken away from her. The danger of being back in the palace was that she'd get dragged back into that superficial existence of personal appearances and mentions in the tabloids. It was that world that had killed her brother, Freddie, and she wanted to do something more substantial and meaningful with her life. She simply didn't know what that was any more. Not while she was like this. Half the person she used to be.

Georgiana slowed her speed for the cooldown phase of her workout and pulled off the headphones. As she stepped back down onto the gym floor, her good leg was trembling with the exertion of her punishing exercise. It knocked her a little off balance and she had to reach out for the nearby chair to steady herself, before collapsing into it, taking the weight off her unsteady prosthetic leg. She'd suffer for this later, knowing the pressure of the prosthesis rubbing on what was left of her lower limb would leave the skin raw. Not that she would feel sorry for herself when she was lucky to still be alive.

'You really shouldn't be so hard on your body.' A critical masculine voice startled her and she reacted as she would with anyone who dared to trespass on her private training session.

'Who are you and how did you get in here?' She stood up so she wasn't at such a disadvantage against the tall, broad figure walking towards her. Squaring up to this stranger wearing only her racer-back gym top and shorts exposing her prosthetic leg wasn't as intimidating as she wanted since it didn't halt his progress towards her.

She was trying not to freak out but wished she hadn't dismissed all the staff in the vicinity. Her fight back to recovery wasn't a spectator sport for anyone, including security or whoever this was. It wouldn't be the first time they'd had an intruder at the palace, thankfully there out of curiosity rather than for any malicious reason. That didn't make a possible similar situation any less concerning.

He didn't look like a tourist who'd walked in off the street, dressed in an immaculate charcoal-grey suit, complete with silver silk tie and real leather shoes. She prayed he wasn't a journalist either. That would almost be worse than someone simply wanting a selfie with a member of the royal family. Her army training had taught her how to defend herself but it was something she hadn't put into practice since her traumatic injury and she didn't want to test it now.

'I'm Edward Lawrence. I was here for a consultation with your mother regarding her riding accident. Sorry for the intrusion. I just happened to see you in here as I was on my way out.'

'And you wanted a closer look at the freak show?' She didn't bother introducing herself. He didn't deserve to be on the receiving end of social niceties if he couldn't observe them himself.

He frowned as though he didn't quite understand her meaning and she waited, arms folded, until the penny dropped.

'Goodness, no. I was taking an interest merely from a professional point of view. I'm a consultant spinal surgeon and physical rehabilitation is one of the specialities at our mobility clinic.' He reached into his inside pocket and produced a business card for Move, a private clinic, presuming she'd accept it as proof of his credentials. His name did ring a bell.

'I haven't been home in quite a while but I remember a Dr Lawrence here as an older, more distinguished gentleman.' One who would've knocked before walking in. He'd been a tall man but with a thinning silver pate and a bushy moustache. A contrast to the sun-kissed swoop of hair this guy was sporting, blond with a matching golden smile on his handsome, clean-shaven face.

'That was my father, a GP. He's retired now.'

If she'd wondered how someone who

would've looked more at home running bare-foot across a beach with a surfboard under his arm had wangled a gig at the palace, now she knew. Nepotism. Regardless of whatever capacity her family had acquired his services, it was nothing to do with her.

'Yes, well, neither you nor your father have any right to be in my personal space so I'd ap-preciate you leaving.' She attempted to show him out with a wave of her hand, uncomfort-able at being exposed to anyone like this.

Since returning home she'd purposely avoided contact with the outside world so her current state would remain unknown or at least a mystery to those with an insatiable appetite for royal scandal. Unveiling her bro-ken body was something she wanted to do at her own pace, if at all. By barging in here un-invited he'd stolen some of that power from her and now she just wanted him gone.

Yet again he showed a blatant disregard for common courtesy by failing, not only to leave, but to apologise. 'By overexerting yourself you're putting your body under more strain. You could be causing more damage. Surely you have some sort of exercise plan drawn up with a physiotherapist?'

His whole lack of manners and apparent knowledge of her circumstances disoriented her. If he knew who she was or had been taken by surprise by her injury he gave no indication of it. His focus remained on how she was potentially abusing her body. Perhaps he was who he purported to be after all. An expert.

'To put your mind at ease, I completed my rehabilitation at a professional residential facility. I'm quite capable of continuing my recovery at home. On my own.'

'Georgiana—I hope I can call you that—' Mystery solved. He knew exactly who he was dealing with and presumably had some idea of how she'd come to be in this position.

He didn't wait for a reply. 'Recovery is an ongoing process best served by remaining in contact with medical professionals. It's a guess but I suspect you haven't attended any follow-up appointments since leaving the centre?'

The truth burned her skin. 'Look, you obviously know who I am, so you'll understand why I'm not keen on continuing my recovery in public. I've got everything I need here. I'm fine.'

He gave her gym equipment a cursory glance. 'No offence but this looks like it's been commissioned by an interior designer, not by anyone who knows what they're doing.'

She should've been offended by the comment. He had absolutely no right to be in her private gym, much less mock it. However, she could see his point. It was the most expensive gym furniture on the market but she had wondered if it had been chosen primarily for decorative reasons. Rehabilitation wasn't meant to be pretty, but the area that had been commandeered for her recovery had been set up before her return. She'd had no input and there had been no consultation with regard to her individual needs. Most likely because her mother didn't trust her judgement over an outsider's on the matter. As a result, she'd been greeted with a room befitting a princess with a gym habit rather than a wounded soldier.

The full-length mirrors she needed to watch her gait were gilded with golden frames. The walls were brilliant white, the floors bleached oak. Perfect for a glossy magazine photo shoot. While she enjoyed the anonymity provided by being in the farthest corner of the palace, it was stark with no natural light coming in. A window wouldn't have gone amiss.

There was a crystal chandelier hanging from the ceiling, dappling the plump, uphol-

mother and daughter. A parent should be able to demonstrate concern for a child without fear of losing them. It was the close bond he had with his own parents that had saved their family. Even if it sometimes felt as if he'd sacrificed his freedom to keep everyone together.

Meeting Georgiana himself, he could understand her mother's reticence to be seen as interfering. She was a force to be reckoned with. Defensive and self-assured, and someone who could totally do this on her own if she had to. It simply made sense to use the services available to aid a faster recovery process. If only her body language didn't scream, 'Stay away from me if you value your life!'

Despite her obvious disability she still had that in-built alertness that came with being a soldier. One false move and he had no doubt she'd battle anyone or anything that threatened her. She certainly looked like a warrior, as well as having that defensive attitude that emanated from her in waves. Her slight frame was toned with defined muscles that would put most people to shame. Eyes blazed with green fire in her heart-shaped face, her defiant chin tilted upward. The flowing brunette locks he'd seen in newspaper features had been shorn into an edgy cut. One side of her head was shaved close to the scalp, while the other was choppy and non-conformist. He wouldn't be surprised if she'd done it herself in a fit of pique. It made her look like the rebel she was reputed to be. The addition of a prosthetic right leg only added to that intimidating impression of someone who was not to be messed with.

Georgiana Ashley was unlike anyone he'd ever met, though he'd come across many other wounded veterans unwilling to appear helpless or weak by accepting help.

'Even if I did agree to scoping the place out, there's the small matter of leaving here unnoticed. It's impossible. I'm sure you've witnessed the crowds of tourists and press assembled outside waiting for a glimpse of life beyond the palace gates.' She clutched her hands to her heart in mock dramatic fashion. Ed was sure the deprecating humour was an attempt to undermine the high esteem the family name drew rather than making fun of those who looked up to them.

'You are the country's main tourist attraction.' He couldn't help adding fuel to the fire and wasn't surprised to receive her narrow-eyed glare in response.

'My point exactly,' she said, letting him get

away with the insolent comment that could have seen him lose his head a few centuries ago.

'If you were serious about attending the clinic, I'm sure we could find some way to get you there.'

'I don't see how, unless you've got an invisibility cloak on you.' She turned her back on him to retrieve a garish set of pink headphones from the treadmill, losing interest in the conversation. Clearly underestimating the heights of his own determination.

'If you're serious, I could sneak you out in my car. No one seems interested in my comings and goings. It shouldn't be too hard to smuggle you out under cover of darkness. That way you could be sure to have the facilities to yourself too, if you attended in the evening.' It might sound like the plot of a farcical movie but Ed was a problem-solver and this seemed the easiest way out of her predicament. If she wasn't simply making excuses.

'Are you joking?' It did manage to grab her attention again and when she faced him, he could see the trace of a smile on her lips.

'I never joke about my work,' he replied in complete seriousness. This wasn't about having a little excitement in his life. Goodness knew he had his hands full already, taking care of his parents and his little brother.

'You would actually try and sneak me out?' She was openly laughing at him now but he didn't care. He would do whatever it took to get her to agree to some sort of aftercare. Not only had he made a promise to her mother but, having spoken to Georgiana, he knew she needed this. A space away from the pressures of her life here and somewhere she could be comfortable in her own skin. To reach the limits he knew she could be capable of now he'd seen her in action. It was their job at the clinic to encourage patients back to full health physically and mentally. Shutting herself off completely from the rest of the world wasn't conducive to that recovery.

'Sure. It's not as if I'd be kidnapping you. If we got stopped, I'd expect you to say as much. I'm not getting locked up for attempted regicide or treason or whatever trumped-up charges they'd come up with.'

'What are we talking here? A blanket over the head or full trench-coat-and-moustache disguise?' At least she'd stopped scowling at him as the idea seemed increasingly to amuse her. It shouldn't be this hard for a person to leave their own home.

'Wear what you want. I'm not your stylist.'

He shrugged, unwilling to make such a big deal of things that she might become wary.

'You have no idea, do you? I mean, why should you? You can just swan around the place as though you've every right to be here simply because your father got you this job.'

'That's not—' His father had mentioned his name for the consultation but he was sure his reputation and experience would have secured the queen's trust in him regardless.

'It must be nice to go where you want, do as you please, with no one expecting anything from you.' She was unleashing some of her frustration on him. It was good, he supposed, for her. Except she knew nothing about his life or the demands upon him. He had no more freedom than her, the princess imprisoned by her own privilege.

If she had the first clue about his situation, she'd never accuse him of having any sort of liberation from family. Not now and especially not when he was growing up. As the eldest of his six siblings, including a brother with spina bifida, he'd shouldered a lot of responsibility. That family loyalty hadn't lessened with age. Most of his brothers and sisters had moved on or married and started families of their own. Things most people took for granted when they pictured their future. Not Ed. He'd stayed close to home, remained in that role of carer, so now he was the one looking after their elderly parents and checking in on his kid brother. That didn't leave room for whatever fun and games Ms Ashley seemed to think he got up to. It had already cost him a relationship of his own.

'That's a lot to assume about someone you don't know.' He was the one getting defensive now.

'We're taught in the army to make quick, detailed assessments of every situation.' She looked him up and down. 'I stand by every word I said.'

Ed bit the inside of his cheek lest he say something he'd later come to regret when he was locked away in a tower somewhere as punishment. 'Thankfully, my offer isn't conditional on your knowledge, or lack thereof, about my personal life. So, if you could set aside whatever preconceived notions and ill-judged prejudice you have against me and focus on yourself, you'll see how you could benefit from our state-of-the-art facility.'

'Uh-huh, and what's in it for you?' Georgiana stripped off her shirt, so she was standing there in only her black sports bra and shorts. He knew it was a move to make him uncomfortable and at the same time display her own confidence. It worked on both levels but he wasn't a man to give up easily.

'Nothing except the satisfaction of giving someone else the best chance of a full recovery. It's what I do.' He knew he sounded glib but he didn't think sincerity was going to do him any favours with her. Those barriers she'd put up weren't coming down any time soon and he could tell straight away she wasn't the sort of woman who'd respond to a softly-softly approach.

She rolled her eyes as she patted a towel around her neck and her décolletage where perspiration from her workout was glistening on her pale skin. If they'd met at a gym or anywhere other than a royal palace, he would never have believed her to be a princess. He was just as guilty of having preconceived notions of her before meeting. Of course, he'd seen and heard mention of her in the press but assumed the stories were either fiction or she was simply another rich kid feigning rebellion. Now he knew different. Georgiana was very much her own person.

He watched as she hooked her thumbs into the waistband of her shorts, tugging them down slightly so the flat plane of her impressive abdominal muscles was visible. It showed she was a hard worker, motivated in the hardest of circumstances to keep up her fitness regime, and boded well for her future despite her life-changing injury.

She cleared her throat and he lifted his eyes to meet her querying gaze.

'If you don't mind, I'd like to shower and change in private.'

'Yes. Sorry.' He bumbled around, trying to avert his gaze and regather his composure.

'Close the door on your way out.' She was ending the conversation and the meeting without agreeing to anything. Ed had to admire her tenacity. It could be the very thing to get her back to the person she used to be. If that was different from the woman standing before him now, he had no idea.

'She's going to be okay, by the way. In case you were wondering.' It occurred to him she hadn't referenced the reason he was in her home in the first place.

'Who?' She looked genuinely puzzled as to who or what he was referring to. It said a lot, nothing good, about her relationship with her mother. Either she didn't care or there had been a complete lack of information shared with her about the accident. Perhaps even both. The concept was alien to someone who was constantly in contact and, indeed, worried about his own parents. His family was always foremost in his thoughts.

'Your mother. Very badly bruised after the fall from her horse but no long-term damage,' he reminded her, in case the details had slipped from her memory during the course of their discussion.

'Oh,' was all the response she mustered. He couldn't help but wonder what had caused their relationship to become so strained. Especially at a time when she would need the support of her family more than ever. He didn't know how she'd got this far without them.

'Anyway, I've checked all the scans and X-rays to put her mind at rest and she's going to be fine,' he assured her again. Although nothing in her tone suggested it had caused her any concern thus far.

If Georgiana, by any miracle, did agree to attend the clinic, he'd be advising her to seek the services of one of their counsellors. In case the psychological trauma had in some way caused this apparent lack of empathy towards the very person who'd come to him for help. Families were a complicated business and no one knew that better than he did.

'I never doubted it. Now, if you don't mind...' She dismissed him again with a nod of her head towards the door. Clearly, social etiquette wasn't as important to her as it was to her mother. Unless this was another side effect from her accident. Sometimes patients had no filter after such an ordeal. She'd been through a lot and he was prepared to make allowances for someone he really knew nothing about. He could only hope she would do the same for him, since he didn't seem to be making a great first impression.

'You have my number should you decide to use our clinic. Goodbye, Miss Ashley.' He turned to take his leave, only to have a pair of shorts land on top of his head.

Unwilling to give her the satisfaction of going back to confront her, clad now only in her underwear, he pulled them off his head and kept walking.

She really didn't know him at all if she thought he wasn't up to a challenge.

CHAPTER TWO

'LET ME TAKE that in for you.' Georgiana reached out to take the silver tray from the maid she'd just startled in the hallway.

'Are you sure, miss?' The wide-eyed girl looked at the tea tray and back at Georgiana, unsure about what to do in the circumstances.

She was a new face, not one Georgiana had seen before being deployed. It was difficult to tell if she was worried her employer's daughter couldn't manage the task without falling over or if she was afraid of letting someone else do her job.

In the end Georgiana made the decision for her and took the tray off her hands. 'I want to check and make sure Mother is okay.'

That seemed enough to ease her conscience and she gave a little curtsey before scuttling off downstairs. It was difficult to get used to being waited on hand and foot after being self-sufficient for so long in the army. From the outset of her return Georgiana had done her best to put an end to that kind of attention and intrusion from the staff by insisting she be left alone. Other than those she ran into in the halls, or in the kitchen when she was on a snack hunt, she rarely had any interaction. It was her way of keeping perspective even though she was living in a palace with servants available at the ring of a bell.

She knocked lightly on her mother's bedroom door.

'Come in.'

Georgiana opened the door with her elbow and slowly backed into the room, careful not to upend the tray. If she made a scene here, it would only prove to her mother she was incapable of the smallest of tasks. Months ago, she could only dream of being able to balance a tea tray without spilling anything. Sheer determination and the stubborn streak she wished her poor brother had inherited had got her to this point. Hopefully, it would be enough to see her through this and back to the life she'd made for herself away from this fake reality. She believed it was better for her mental health if she was able to live independently from her parents again, where she was able to think for herself and not under pressure to live the way they wanted her to.

'I thought I'd come and see what the consultant said.' She couldn't be sure if it was guilt or anger that had kept the man and his comments in her thoughts while she'd changed.

'Georgiana, you shouldn't be carrying that. Where did that girl go? I wish Lise had never left. At least she knew how to do her job properly.' Her mother shifted up the bed, struggling to sit upright but somehow still managing to look regal in her nightgown.

'I sent her away. I wanted to bring you your tea.' She placed the tray across the patient's knees and arranged the pillows behind her until she was sure her mother was comfortable.

'You shouldn't be doing that in your condition.'

'I'm not pregnant, Mother, and I don't have a condition. I've had an amputation and I need to adjust to it, not pretend it hasn't happened.' This was the kind of thing she usually tried to avoid—a pity party thrown in her honour. She didn't want one and she didn't deserve one. It was her parents' refusal to accept what was going on before their very eyes that had resulted in Freddie taking his own life. If the family had pulled together, faced the future united and been honest to themselves and the rest of the world, he might still be here.

'You shouldn't be pushing yourself too hard.'

Where had she heard that one before?

'I'm not. I'm only bringing you some tea,' she said with a smile, trying to give her mother the benefit of the doubt that she was truly worried about her daughter's health and not wrapped up in how her disabled daughter would look to the staff.

'We have employees to do that, dear.'

'So, Mr Lawrence says you're going to be okay. That's good news.' Georgiana pulled over a chair and sat down, her muscles beginning to ache after her workout.

'Oh, you saw him?' There was a sparkle in her mother's eyes at the mere mention of the handsome consultant. Georgiana could admit the dashing Edward Lawrence was something of a head turner because it would be a long time before she acted on any attraction to the opposite sex. If ever. Especially if it was someone so rude and pushy as the aforementioned visitor.

A memory of her attempt at having the last say popped into her head. The absolute gall of him to take her shorts with him as some sort of trophy. It went to show the difference between him and his distinguished father. He wasn't embarrassed at all by her undressing in front of him. It certainly hadn't hastened his exit as she'd intended.

'Hmm… He stopped by the gym. Where did you get him from anyway? He seems very full of himself, if you ask me.' She was still smarting after their encounter. Primarily because he seemed to think he knew her body better than she did.

'His father retired a few years ago but he came very highly recommended. Edward has a lovely bedside manner.'

'I'm sure he does,' she muttered, not having had the same experience.

'He can be very discreet, if that's what you're worried about, darling.' She gave a pointed look towards Georgiana's prosthetic. It was difficult to admit that her mother was correct in her assumption that having him see her was what had bothered her.

'I think you might need to talk to him about boundaries. Surely he shouldn't be free to wander around here snooping on the rest of us if it's you he's here to see.' If he wasn't intimidated in the slightest by her, admonishment from the monarch might take him down a peg or two. His ego could do with some deflating.

'I—I'll have a word with him. Did he say something to upset you, Georgiana?'

'He…uh…'

It wasn't so much what he'd said to her, more the way he'd said it. All superior and cocky. Although she knew if she said that, she'd sound like a petulant brat and her mother didn't need more reason to treat her like a child. It was one of those things she'd simply have to deal with and move on.

'Not exactly. He said I was welcome to use the gym equipment at his clinic. In his opinion it's better than the stuff I'm using at home and could speed my recovery.' When she said it out loud it seemed so straight-forward. That was what she wanted, wasn't it? To get back to normal as soon as possi-ble. Perhaps if anyone other than the laid-back Mr Lawrence had offered, she wouldn't have been so against the initial idea. Now she was beginning to wonder if she'd let her per-sonal opinion of the man in question cloud her judgement. If she stripped away the per-sonality traits that made her dislike him on sight and focused on the professional interest, she could see they both had the same goal in mind. To get her back to her fighting best.

'That's good, isn't it?' Hope was written all over her mother's face that this was somehow the answer to all their prayers. As though some high-grade gym equipment would restore her to the woman she was before her injury. For once Georgiana and her mother were in complete agreement about what they wanted.

'Have you completely lost your mind?'

Ed glanced up from his laptop to find his business partner, Giles Winhope, sitting on his desk. 'You got my message, then? I'd appreciate it if you kept the details between us. I promised full confidentiality.'

'And you didn't think to consult me before you agreed to this?'

'You were on board with our other royal appointment. I didn't think it would be a problem.'

'You wouldn't,' Giles muttered as he sorted Ed's paperwork into a pile and rounded up the assortment of dirty coffee cups he hadn't got around to washing yet.

Okay, he had a casual approach to housekeeping, but he gave everything important in his life his full attention. It was no reason to accuse him of being unprofessional.

'It's one thing having royal approval from the queen, but agreeing to sneak her daughter in here isn't exactly standard business practice.'

Ed had been as surprised as anyone when Georgiana had called. He'd extended the invitation but he hadn't expected to hear from her after their meeting unless it was to demand her shorts back. In hindsight it was possible he'd taken them home with him so she would have reason to speak to him again. Even if it was to threaten him with the police. Except she hadn't mentioned them at all during the short phone call, sticking only to the salient points.

'I'd like to take you up on your offer of using the facilities at your clinic. In private. Pick me up tomorrow night at seven o'clock.' She hadn't given him the chance to speak, much less remind her that he wasn't one of her servants. He had promised to transport her in relative privacy but he wasn't at her beck and call. Something he'd point out to her at the first opportunity. He had family commitments, which came before everything else.

'To be honest, I never thought she'd agree. It was her mother who thought she needed some extra encouragement.'

'It's going to be a circus around here. Are we going to have to get extra security to accommodate our new client? A press room? Souvenir stalls?' Giles's main concern was always money. He and Ed were polar opposites but that was what made them such good business partners. Ed was the heart and soul of the clinic while Giles was the money man. Neither minded admitting their strengths and weaknesses because between them they made it work. Along with the other consultants, doctors, nurses and assorted staff they employed.

When the call had first come in for Ed to have a consultation at the palace, Giles had been over the moon because it added a certain gravitas to their reputation. Those who moved in the same aristocratic circles as the Ashleys would know they were the best at what they did now they had royal patronage. That prestige added financial value to the team. It was the thought of having to pay money out to oblige Georgiana that was causing him to come out in a sweat.

If Ed was a cruel man, he'd continue to let Giles think their finances were about to take a massive hit. Fortunately, he wasn't.

'Ms Ashley wants to remain incognito. No staff, no press, no other gym users when she's here.'

'How are we going to manage that? That

will seriously damage our appointment book.' That was Giles's speak for losing income.

'I said we'd open exclusively for her at night. I'm a keyholder, I can arrange it, don't worry.' It was on his head since he was the one to suggest the move without proper consultation with the rest of the team.

'How are you going to manage that along with your other personal commitments?' Giles arched an eyebrow in disbelief that he could make this work but Ed wasn't one to shirk his responsibilities.

He had surgery days at the local hospital as well as his work here at the clinic and just as many demands on him at home. The only time he'd let anyone down was in his personal life when he'd failed to carve out enough time and energy to save his relationship with his ex, Caroline. He'd thought he could settle down like anyone else but when she'd left him he'd realised there was only room for one family in his life. It hadn't really been a choice for him, when he'd always be there for his parents, but it still hurt.

Worse than his own heartbreak was knowing he'd caused Caroline so much pain in the process. She'd done nothing wrong except get involved with someone who couldn't give her everything she needed. Ed had sworn then not to get into another serious relationship and repeat the same mistake.

He regretted not being there for Caroline as much as everyone else in his life but it made it easier to manage his other commitments now he was single.

'That's up to me to figure out. This is a done deal, Giles. I'm on my way to pick her up now. I'm simply doing you the courtesy of letting you know what's going on.'

'After the fact…'

'I didn't get much notice myself, to be fair, but she needs this. It's what we do.' He grabbed his car keys off the desk and shrugged on his jacket. There was no point in picking holes in things now, when he'd made arrangements. He simply needed Giles gone before he brought Georgiana here.

'So, you're doing chauffeur and personal trainer?' Giles shifted himself off the desk with a sigh of resignation. This was happening whether he liked it or not.

'I'm not sure how much input she's going to want from me or anyone else with regard to her training, but she doesn't want anyone to know she's attending. That makes me chauffeur, escort and bodyguard, I guess.'

They both headed for the exit. Ed decided

against turning the lights off since he'd be back within the hour.

'Are you sure you can manage this on your own?' Giles asked.

Ed thought about the fearsome Georgiana, who looked permanently ready to go into battle, and shrugged his shoulders. 'I guess we'll find out.'

Georgiana checked her watch for the umpteenth time. He was late. Every extra second she waited here, the more her stomach somersaulted and her breathing quickened.

It had been weeks since she'd been beyond the palace gates and if Mr Lawrence didn't get here soon there was every chance she'd change her mind about doing this. She supposed it wasn't a big deal to him; she doubted anything was. To her, though, this could be the start of her new life. Or the first time her secret might be exposed to the outside world.

She texted him.

Where are you?

Since the initial phone call to confirm her attendance, she'd kept contact limited to text messages with instructions of when and where to pick her up. Though she was keeping her nocturnal visit quiet from the public, she was keen to keep it from those inside the palace too. There was no way they'd agree to her leaving without security. Whether Edward didn't realise the risks they were taking, or he didn't care, he'd gone along with the plan. Which entailed smuggling her out under the noses of security and the staff. The logistics of which were not easy and only added to her swelling anxiety.

I'm here. Out the back. Where we arranged.

She'd got him security clearance, citing a medical consultation so he wouldn't seem suspicious turning up here. The plan was for her to slip out the back unseen and he would drive her out, leaving security none the wiser. It was very cloak and dagger but she'd rather do it this way than go through formal procedures to authorise the visit.

She'd dressed down, in dark clothes so she didn't draw attention to herself. With a baseball cap pulled low, she crept out into the courtyard where Edward was waiting for her.

He was standing with his hands in his pockets staring up at the night sky. His profile was romantically lit by the moon, defining his strong jaw and the sparkle of his eyes.

He'd ditched his tie and his shirt was open at the collar. Clearly it hadn't occurred to him to keep up appearances once he'd clocked off work.

Her breath hitched in her throat but it was due to the thrill of sneaking out, nothing else. The last time she'd done anything like this was with Freddie when they were kids. He'd been the bad influence then and she should've encouraged that independent streak instead of trying to tame it along with everyone else. If they'd all simply let him be who he was without imposing stupid restrictions on him he might still be here.

The crunch of gravel under her feet drew Edward's attention, a genuine smile on his face appearing when he saw her. Thinking about her brother and all the time they should have had together made her too sad to return it. She was angry Freddie wasn't here to make jokes at her expense and be the light during the darkest time of her life. At least, the darkest one since her dear brother had ended his life.

That hadn't been the official cause of death but she knew, as did her parents, that he'd killed himself rather than continue living a lie. The tragedy of that being that they were still living that lie to save face. That betrayal of Freddie's memory had proved the final straw and the turning point in her own life. Determined not to end up in the same position as Freddie, forced to be someone she wasn't, Georgiana had joined the army. It was the best decision she'd ever made but she hadn't counted on being injured and forced to return home, in a more vulnerable position now than when she'd left.

'You're late,' she snapped, unwilling to let him see any weakness in the tears she was holding back at the thought of the injustice done to her and Freddie. Edward's smile narrowed by the second.

'Only by fifteen minutes. I had to run things by my business partner before I left. This was a bit last minute, you know. I do have a life away from here.' Apparently, it was his turn to vent some irritation and she knew she deserved it. Georgiana found it reassuring that she could ruffle his feathers as much as he could hers. She might've disturbed him on a date or a night out with the lads. Whatever counted as a life for a single man in his late thirties.

'Let's go before someone spots us.' She went to open the back door of his car but Edward hovered beside her.

'You're getting in there?'

'I'm not about to climb into the boot.' She rapped her knuckles on her lower leg, letting the hollow sound explain the reason why.

'Oh. Yes. Sorry.' Thankfully he went to retrieve something from the boot so she was able to get into the back seat unseen. Although she'd mastered the art of walking again, things such as climbing into the back of a car could be tricky. Ungainly. She didn't want him to see her struggling and feel sorry for her. It was much easier to deal with those who either pretended not to notice her disability or who didn't care about it. People she'd found were few and far between.

'If you want to lie down, I've got a blanket I can put over you.' He came back with a tartan picnic rug and a box of files.

'Do you do a lot of this, Mr Lawrence?' She couldn't help but tease in an attempt to cover her own unease at the situation. The occupational therapist had helped her deal with transferring her body weight in and out of seats during rehab, but this was the first time she'd done it in front of a relative stranger. That slight struggle to manoeuvre herself into the small space reminded her of her limitations and it wasn't something she relished.

'Not often, no.' He didn't rise to the bait. It obviously took more than gentle teasing to embarrass him or else he did have a habit of entertaining random women in the back of his car.

The thought of which suddenly made her black hoodie and sweatpants combo too warm against her skin. It didn't help when he covered her with the blanket so she couldn't be seen from outside.

'I'm going to set some of my files on you to help cover the fact there's a body under there.'

There was a gentle pressure as he weighted her down with paperwork, then she heard the door slam when he was finished. The car suspension adjusted to take his weight when he got in the driver's seat and the engine purred into life. It was pitch black under her disguise and claustrophobic. Her hot breath came in gasps, increasing the temperature and her unease as they drove off.

There was that same trepidation she used to experience before going out on patrol with her unit, not knowing what lay outside the safety of the compound. Sure, this wasn't a life or death situation but the adrenaline rush and fear of the unknown brought back memories of that horrific day. Perspiration coated her skin and she was doing her best to quell the panic threatening to reveal her to the outside world. She was seconds away from whipping the blanket off and winding down the window to gulp some fresh air.

'Are you all right back there?' As if he'd sensed her discomfort, Edward's voice filtered through her claustrophobia to provide a grounding reassurance. He was a medical professional; he knew what she'd been through and if there was the slightest chance she was freaking out he'd be the first to call a halt to this.

She took deep, long cleansing breaths and visualised the freedom afforded her outside the gates. No prying eyes, whispered conversations or sympathetic stares. It was enough to steel her through the next leg of the journey.

'I'm fine.' Her muffled voice didn't project as well as she'd hoped.

If he had any doubts about her state of mind or what they were doing, he said nothing and kept driving. She suspected he was leaving it down to her to make the crucial decisions. It made a nice change not having someone taking over and telling her what was in her best interests.

The car slowed, she heard the electric window go down and muffled voices outside. He'd reached the security gate where they were probably giving the visitor and his car another sweep before he left the palace.

Georgiana held her breath, illogically thinking they could somehow hear her as they walked around the car. Every footstep, every pause in between, convinced her she was about to be rumbled. Then she heard a double thump on the roof, some more deep muttering before the car set off again.

''Bye,' she heard Edward call cheerfully and she could imagine him waving to the guards on the way past.

As soon as the electric window whirred back to life, she was able to breathe again.

'You really should up the security around here,' Edward said for her benefit.

'I'll look into that.' She hoped he could tell she was rolling her eyes at him under here. 'Can I come out yet?'

She hated being literally kept in the dark. Not knowing what was going on around her, blind to the surroundings and relying on someone else to keep her safe.

'I'll do a few laps around these side streets and make sure no one is following us first.'

'Okay.' She'd forgotten it wasn't simply about getting out undiscovered but also dodging any press lurking around. Crawling out of the back of a car really would get her in the headlines and in everyone else's bad books.

Patience. It was something she'd had to have a lot of recently and didn't come easily to her. She wanted to be back to normal *now*. Not when her stupid body was ready. She didn't want to think about what would happen if her physical self never caught up with her determined mind.

The click of the indicator and the car slowing brought her back to the present.

'I think it's safe for you to come out now. You can stay in the back if you want or sit up here in the passenger seat like a commoner.' Edward's sarcasm was a welcome distraction from her own thoughts and worries.

'Do you think I drove around Afghanistan with a chauffeur?' she snarked back, throwing off her coverings.

'No. I assumed you travelled with your golden carriage and horses.'

'They don't work so well in the desert and tend to draw attention.'

Edward waited with the engine idling for her to join him in the front of the car. She was grateful he didn't get out to offer her a hand, preferring to manage on her own.

The cold night air went some way to regulating her body temperature again, so she was relatively comfortable for the remainder of the journey.

'I thought we should go in the back door to avoid detection,' he said, pulling up outside the clinic. It wasn't too far from the palace, making the whole escapade easier.

'This must be a novelty for you.'

'What?' It was all new to her—sneaking around, getting out of the palace and being around someone who wasn't family or military.

'Using the tradesman's entrance. I imagine you're used to red carpets and the smell of fresh paint everywhere you go.'

'You mean you haven't been redecorating to an appropriate standard for my arrival? Tut-tut.' Getting out of the front of the car was slightly easier so she wasn't as defensive as she was earlier. In fact she was almost beginning to enjoy her time out with the consultant. He wasn't as annoying when not telling her what to do or making out he knew what was best for her. How long that would last now they were in his territory, she had no idea.

'As I said, this was late notice or, you know, we would've held a reception for you.' He countered her sarcasm with some of his own and opened up the clinic, leaving Georgiana to get out of the car on her own.

She wondered if this was how he behaved around most women or if this was just for her. He looked like a door opener, a 'take a woman's hand and help her out of the car' gentleman. She thought more of him for sparing her blushes and realising she'd hate him to do that for her. That courteous gesture in other circumstances wouldn't have bothered her but these days it simply reminded her she couldn't do the simple things on her own.

Given their short history there was a possibility he was just rude in keeping his back to her until she managed to get back on her feet.

'How did your partner take the news about me using this place out of hours?' She wasn't so obtuse she didn't realise this was unorthodox and the clinic wouldn't get the publicity they'd probably otherwise prefer. Edward had mentioned being late because of their meeting and Georgiana hoped she wasn't the cause of any fallout.

Now she paused to think about it, having her here would be more of a headache than a bonus to their business. It made her wonder why on earth Edward had suggested it. Especially when she'd taken him for the type to avoid any hassle that could impede his freedom.

'He's fine with it. As long as I'm the one putting in the extra hours to accommodate our new guest.' He flashed her a smile as he let her into the premises to show her he didn't mind. It only served to make her feel worse about the way she'd treated him thus far when he was going out of his way to accommodate her.

They'd come to a compromise over her use of the equipment so there was no misunderstanding over their roles here. She wasn't going to be a paying client, thus Edward wouldn't have any input into what she was doing. There would be no doctor/patient relationship. This was a favour.

Whatever his reasons, it was difficult for her to believe anyone could be so altruistic. She'd been through so much, trust wasn't something she gave easily. Life with her parents had made her guarded and her injuries had made her even more so. In the army she'd been forced to rely on others, at times put her life in their hands. She'd had to do the same with the hospital team who'd saved her after the blast. This was different and Edward was still virtually a stranger. Surely, she was right to be wary?

She could thank him, tell him not to put himself out on her account but that made it sound as though she owed him something.

'Good. I wouldn't want any disgruntled staff selling me out to the papers to get the clinic some publicity.' She walked on in, doing her best to exude that self-entitled, regal air despite her current outward appearance.

'No. You have my word on that score. Privacy is very important here. Now, let me give you the tour.' The sincere comment combined with his unflinching eye contact made her believe him. That unwavering blue-eyed gaze also caused the hairs to stand up on the back of her neck. For a moment she was lost, swimming in that azure sea without a care in the world. Then he rested his hand on her elbow to gently guide her and jolted her back to the present.

Etiquette around members of the royal family included a 'no touching' rule. One she should be enforcing right now. Except it had been a long time since she'd felt that human connection. In hospital she'd detested being poked and prodded and having her limbs manipulated. No control over her own body. Being back home she'd been so focused on getting better, in private, she'd starved herself of basic human interaction. It was nice to have someone touch her so casually without it being a big issue.

CHAPTER THREE

'WE'VE DONE EXTENSIVE research on the best equipment for someone living with a disability.' Edward was proudly showing off the fitness machines in the shiny gym but his last word was a slap across the face to Georgiana.

She still thought of invalids being those who'd suffered a serious stroke or a spinal-cord injury. Even other people who'd had amputations, but not her. Despite the permanency of her loss she continued to see her situation as a temporary problem she could solve with a lot of hard work. Other people might call it denial but she knew it was her mental strength that would get her back to her physical peak along with the training.

'A lot of this I already have at home.' She picked up one of the dumbbells from the bench with ease. The weights and resistance bands were crucial to strengthening her upper body so she could support those weaker areas during exercise.

'I know, and I'm not saying you should stop your home training. The extra work you do here is to supplement that. We have the arm cycles, for example. There are the free-standing machines you can use with or without seats depending on how much you rely on your wheelchair.'

'I don't need a wheelchair.' She'd hated that thing from the very first moment she'd been pushed around in it like some helpless infant. The one thing it had done for her was to spur her on to her first milestone: to be able to get out of it. Some didn't have an option but knowing she could walk on her own if she worked hard enough had been a powerful motivator. Sure, there were some days she was in pain, when it would be easier to give in and use it for getting mobile. On those bad days she'd use her crutches so there was some support but she still had to work at it.

Edward held his hands up. 'Hey, there's no judgement here and absolutely no shame in using them. A lot of our patients are wheelchair users. Wearing a prosthetic leg places additional stress on the body and you do what you need to in order to stay mobile. I'm simply advising you on the options available.'

Georgiana knew she was being testy but the chip on her shoulder about being seen using one of those things came directly from her mother. They were both aware it marked her out as different when it was possible for her to pull on a pair of trousers so no one would know she wasn't whole.

'I appreciate that but I won't need anything to do with a wheelchair.' It had been difficult enough coming back from rehab to find her parents had adapted half the house for a wheelchair user. As though it was going to be a permanent feature. Well, she'd showed them, putting in the effort to ensure she didn't have to use one longer than necessary. Now the ramps that had been installed for her benefit slowed her up when she had to adjust her balance every time she walked up or down one.

'I'm just giving you the standard tour. Take or leave whatever is or isn't applicable to your specific needs.' He appeared unfazed by the news and Georgiana was miffed by his indifference. It was a huge achievement when someone transitioned back onto their feet and an acknowledgement of that would be nice. Perhaps he was so used to dealing with patients at every level of rehabilitation it wasn't as big a deal to him as it was to her.

'I see you have the heavy boxing bag. I suppose that's for core work.' And relieving frustration, as long as she didn't overbalance in her enthusiasm to punch things.

'Yes, and the speed bag can be adjusted so you're reaching overhead and challenge your range of motion.'

'Hmm. Maybe I'll take up boxing. We're always encouraged to get involved in competitive sport. I like the idea of punching people in the face.' They championed sport to improve fitness but also to give patients a new area of their lives to focus on and work towards. That competitive spirit gave a boost to those who might otherwise want to give up. She wasn't going to be one of those people lying in bed all day feeling sorry for herself, but neither did she want to be on a stage celebrating what had happened to her.

Boxing, however, was a skill she could carry through with her as another defence for when her sardonic repartee failed to get people like Edward Lawrence to back off.

'I'm not sure that's the spirit of the sport. Remind me never to get on the wrong side of you.' Without his jacket she could see the impressive bulge of his biceps straining the cotton shirt and she knew she'd be no challenge to him. Yet she appreciated that he didn't think of her as a fragile doll.

'I do have military training…' She gave him what she hoped was an intimidating glare, although her Cheshire cat impression might have undermined the overall effect.

'I'll bear that in mind,' he said with a grin to match hers. 'Especially when I tell you about the glider here. Yes, it's designed for wheelchair users but I think it does help build the oblique, core, back and arm muscles.'

She pursed her lips to prevent a further tirade about why it wasn't suitable for someone who could get around perfectly fine. He knew that now but he obviously had more to say on the subject.

'Go on…'

The worried frown lines evened out across his forehead when she let him off the hook. 'You can pull up a seat and just work out the arms on this one. It's a great way to improve strength and cardio. Plus, it can strengthen your shoulder orbit muscles.' He demonstrated the machine, pulling and pushing the levers, which she could see were replicating rowing and cross-country skiing motions for the upper body.

She had a rowing machine at home but she had to take off her leg to keep the air flow on her limb and prevent sweating. This glider would certainly complement the exercises she was already doing for her arms. By combining both gym workouts she'd hopefully improve her overall fitness. Edward certainly looked fit. She was mesmerised by his thick, tanned forearms pumping the levers back and forth. That was the level of strength she aspired to. Her fascination wasn't in any way an objectification of the man himself.

'It looks…er…good.' She cleared her throat and her mind. This man was an aid to her recovery, nothing more. Okay, maybe he was some pretty window dressing in a room dominated by ugly, functional machinery.

'Do you need me to demonstrate anything else or help draw up some sort of plan? I know that's not my particular area of expertise but I have learned a thing or two over the years about strength and conditioning exercises.' He walked over to the stationary bike and though her first instinct was to scoff and tell him she knew how to ride one, a different instinct held her back.

'You can change the gradient here depending on how much resistance you want.' He was talking as he pushed the buttons on the electronic display panel but she was more interested in watching the bulging thigh muscles rippling with his every pedal.

'I know how a bike works,' she snapped eventually, not happy about the physical reaction she was having to the scene before her. It wasn't as though she was unused to being in close proximity to men in their prime. She'd been in the army, for goodness' sake, living and fighting along with the best the country had to offer, and she hadn't had her head turned. Yet she couldn't seem to take her eyes off every flex of muscle and wonder what lay beneath the fabric of his clothes.

'We're supposed to run through instructions for the equipment with all new patients but I guess I'm not an instructor and you're not a patient.'

'No. Think of it more as private rental of the space. I'm not here for the social side.' Even if spending time with him tonight had proved an eye-opener for her.

'I don't suppose you'll be needing an exercise programme customised for you either? That could be arranged along with any of our other services.' He swung his leg over the bike and came to join her again. Georgiana knew he meant well but she'd be more at ease once he left her alone.

She shook her head. 'I have all that from

the rehab centre and I'd prefer to adapt things to suit my own body's needs and capabilities. I know my boundaries and how far I can push them.' Cardio and strength training had been her priority since coming home in her effort to get her body back to the way she wanted it. Short of growing her leg back. She didn't need anyone interfering or disrupting her training and slowing her progress.

'Right, well, don't overdo it,' he reiterated, managing to raise her hackles again. 'I'll be working in my office if you need me. Let me know when you're ready to leave.' He pointed to a door down the hallway. Thankfully, it wasn't one of those open-plan, all-glass set-ups, which would have stripped away any illusion of privacy. Once he was secured behind his office door, she was free to do her thing without an audience.

As he made his way off the gym floor, Georgiana followed so she could close the door after him. He caught her off guard when he spun around again. She didn't have time to react and move back, so they were almost nose to nose when he spoke.

'Oh. I was just going to say I didn't have time to show you the pool area. Not to worry. You can't use that without supervision anyway. We'll sort something out for next time.'

He seemed to say everything in one breath, then turned away sharply to disappear down the corridor. Leaving her breathless in his wake.

It took her a few seconds and some deep breaths to absorb what had happened. His usual cool demeanour had deserted him momentarily. Almost as though being so up close in her personal space had thrown him as much as her. She had to concentrate to remember what he'd even said. Something about the pool being out of bounds. It didn't matter tonight as she hadn't brought a swimsuit with her, but the pool had been the clincher for her coming here. She missed swimming but hadn't been able to face doing it in a public area with people staring. A situation where she really couldn't hide any more.

Once Georgiana completed the cool-down part of her workout, she longed for the soothing relief of a warm pool to ease her aches and pains. Hydrotherapy was the one thing she'd looked forward to when she'd been in the rehab unit.

When she'd first slid into the water after her amputation, the sense of movement had been a defining moment in her recovery progress. It was then she'd realised she didn't have to be confined to a wheelchair for the rest of her life.

Her physical therapist had helped her see the benefits of exercising in the water. The warm water relaxed her body and allowed her to become vertical without bearing weight on her remaining leg. It made things more bearable in those early days compared to her land-based regime.

She'd done her cardio now on Edward's expensive toys, so she didn't need to do the deep-water jogging while wearing a flotation belt around her middle, which did the same job. Some sense of normalcy would be nice now, where she didn't have to strap on fake body parts and work hard just to walk. Her mood was completely different when she was in the water because she wasn't consumed by anxiety. She was free to enjoy a swim and move unimpeded. Without pain or fear.

A glance down the hall told her Edward was still ensconced in his office as she undertook a little tour of her own. All she had to do was follow the smell of chlorine. Georgiana had only intended to take a look, get a feel for the place, but the water was so inviting. The low-level evening lighting was preferable to the usual fluorescent glare she was forced to endure when swimming. It was calming and the empty pool was calling for her to take a soothing dip.

She could see they had all the hoists and devices for lowering disabled bodies into the water but she no longer needed any of that. The fact she didn't have a bathing costume didn't put her off either. She simply stripped off at the side of the pool, so she was standing in her neon-pink sports bra and mismatched black knickers. It was removing her leg that made her more self-conscious but with no one here to see she had nothing to worry about.

Using the handrail at the side of the steps, she eased herself in. Once she was enveloped in that watery embrace she could finally relax. On her back now, she floated aimlessly, letting her thoughts drift away. The glittering, morphing reflection of the water on the ceiling hypnotised her into a state of calm. Here, it didn't matter about her appearance or abilities. She could just be.

It was only the occasional splash when her constantly swishing hands keeping her afloat slapped the surface that disturbed her reverie. She could get used to coming here to unwind at night. Edward had indicated she'd need supervision but she wasn't one of those helpless patients who couldn't fend for herself. There'd been a time when she had been dependent on lifeguards and physios to make sure she didn't drown but she'd worked hard to get this independence and she wasn't going to give it up now.

Once she thought her hydrotherapy was bordering on being self-indulgent, she rolled over onto her belly and began to swim. There were those who had special prosthetics made to swim with but she was content to be un-encumbered for this short time.

After a few lengths she began to tire. Her limbs and lungs were telling her they'd had enough for one day. Regardless of what Mr Lawrence thought, she did listen to her body. She wanted to improve and regain the fitness levels she'd had pre-amputation, not make things worse. At this point she didn't know what that could be but if she overdid things there was a fear of being laid up again.

Those weeks spent in hospital, unable to do anything, followed by relearning basic things such as standing and walking, had been the worst time of her life. It had left her weak and ashamed at being so helpless, relying on strangers to help her carry out the simplest tasks. There was no way she was returning to those dark days.

The clock on the far wall told her it was getting late. As kind as Edward had been in staying on, she didn't want to take advantage. He had work in the morning and there was likely to be someone waiting for him at home. Oddly, the thought of him going back to a cosy domestic scene while she sneaked back into the palace, where her disappearance probably wouldn't have been noticed, bugged her.

She hauled herself up and over the edge of the pool where she'd left her clothes. Unfortunately, she hadn't had the foresight to set a towel within reach. There was a bale of freshly laundered fluffy white towels sitting on the low-level lockers over by the door. She had two options: either put her clothes on over her wet underwear or hop over to get one. There was no point trying to put her leg on first when she was wet. She needed to dry off before she attempted that.

It wasn't that far anyway, and she was used to getting around on one leg in her bedroom rather than put the blasted thing on and off when she needed to get something.

With the aid of the handrail, she pulled into an upright position and steadied herself. She propelled herself forward, letting her leg take the full weight of her body. It took a few seconds to centre herself again and get her balance. Things like this were tiring and frustrating. Such was her new norm after a lifetime of taking such a basic thing as having two legs for granted. If she didn't believe things like this would get easier she'd have given up a long time ago.

Another hop brought her closer to her target but as her foot landed on the tiled floor it splashed in a small puddle of water and she lost traction. Though she frantically reached out for anything to stabilise her, she was powerless against gravity and landed with a thud.

The pain was excruciating as she hit the deck. When her body landed on the hard, wet surface it literally knocked the breath out of her. Her head had cracked against the tiles too and she lay there stunned, wondering how things had gone so wrong so quickly.

'Georgiana? What the hell—?' Edward's angry voice reverberated around the walls and for a moment she thought she'd imagined it. Until he loomed over her. She groaned out of pain and the humiliation of him finding her lying here.

'I slipped.' She sounded pathetic and knew she looked even more so, sprawled here with her stump on show for the world to see.

'I've been looking everywhere for you. Did you hurt yourself?' He knelt beside her in the puddle of water. The genuine look of concern on his face as he brushed the wet strands of hair out of her eyes made her want to weep. She loathed seeing sympathy on people's faces yet at the same time she was desperate for someone to see, to realise, what she was going through inside. To confide those feelings in anyone meant trusting again and she wasn't ready for that. She could only stay strong if she listened to herself and didn't rely on others for her happiness.

'It's nothing serious. I've felt worse.' The dark humour was supposed to cover her uncharacteristic bout of self-pity but she could sense her chin wobbling and giving the game away. If Ed showed her any more compassion there was every chance she'd fling her arms around him and cry on his shoulder. The whole scene was mortifying and she was tempted to roll over and let the water claim her.

'This is why I told you not to come here alone. For your own safety.' He reached over to grab a few of the towels and covered her body to keep her warm. Oh, yeah, she was lying here in her wet underwear too. Honestly, she didn't think she could've done a better job of humiliating herself if she'd tried.

'I know… I'm sorry.' She hiccupped, fighting the sobs trying to burst out of her throat.

'All you had to do was ask, Georgiana, and I would've come with you.' The words came out on a sigh, so it sounded less of a scolding and more like disappointment in her. That made it so much worse.

'I know… I'm sorry,' she repeated. Really, what more could she say? This was her fault, not his. All because of her stubborn pride.

She tried to sit up but Edward was having none of it.

'Stay still until I've checked you over.'

'I'm sure I'll be fine,' she insisted as he gently felt her head for signs of injury.

'There's no sign of any blood and I don't see any abrasions. Did you lose consciousness at any time?'

'No. I don't feel sick or have any problems with my vision either. I'm pretty sure I don't have a concussion.' She was able to diagnose herself even if he wouldn't take her word for it.

'It doesn't mean you couldn't develop symptoms later. I'll get you an ice pack to stop any swelling developing and you can rest up in my office for a while where I can keep an eye on you.'

'I don't need looking after. I can manage on my own.' She struggled to sit up to prove her point but Ed didn't budge from her side.

'What is your problem? Why are you so against anyone helping you? Or is it just me?'

With his piercing eyes locked onto her, Georgiana had nowhere to hide from his questions. He had every right to be annoyed with her. She'd kept him up all night, ignored his warning about coming here alone and now he was the one left picking up the pieces. That was how she saw herself now—broken pieces of the woman she used to be and someone who could never be repaired. Not that she could voice any of that to him when it sounded so pathetic.

Unfortunately, those emotions she'd been supressing for so long bubbled to the surface because of this one act of kindness. Instead of giving him an answer or a snappy comeback to cover her embarrassment, she burst into messy, ugly tears.

'Georgiana? I didn't mean to upset you. Sorry. Please don't cry.' Ed thought he couldn't feel any worse than he had when he'd seen her lying on the floor in pain. Now he'd made this strong, seemingly fearless Amazon sob into his chest by shouting at her.

She seemed so fragile and vulnerable in his arms and, though he liked having her there, he hated the idea of her being so upset.

Georgiana wasn't a woman who showed her emotions easily. Unless it was to express her dislike towards him. Although now he was beginning to wonder if he'd got that wrong about her too.

He should've been keeping a closer eye on her. Instead he'd had his head buried in paperwork for a cause he was having difficulty getting off the ground. If Georgiana had been anyone else here he would've insisted on being involved in their training regime but there was something about her that made him go against all his instincts. He could tell she needed to do things on her own but he shouldn't have let that compromise her safety.

Now she was hurt and embarrassed, desperately trying to cover her leg as though he hadn't already seen it. Naturally it bothered him to see it but from a personal point of view, not for any aesthetic reason. It was an indication of the amount of suffering she'd gone through. Something he'd probably never be able to understand. She was such a strong individual but one slip on a wet tile seemed to have broken her and he knew she'd hate for him to witness it. He had a strong-minded younger brother who was just as determined to manage his disability on his own. Jamie's spina bifida was something he and the family had lived with for his entire life, so Ed knew that sometimes the smallest upset could cause a setback. He was always there to make sure that didn't happen.

'Shh. It's all right,' he soothed, his arm around her, holding her tight to him. 'Everything's going to be all right.'

Georgiana continued to weep into his chest, silently now but with no less sorrow.

In different circumstances he was sure she'd jump on that, demanding to know how things could possibly be all right when she wasn't about to grow her leg back, but for now she seemed content to let him placate her.

Eventually her shoulders stopped heaving with the effort of crying and she withdrew from him.

'I'm so sorry. I don't know what came over me. Shame probably.' She wiped away the tears and offered up a heartbreaking half-smile, trying to dismiss everything he'd just seen.

'There is absolutely no need to be ashamed about anything. Nor do you have to keep pushing me away, Georgiana. I know what your injuries are. I deal with similar every day.' He saw her flinch at the acknowledgement but if that was holding her back from accepting help, they had to address it.

'It—it's something I'm still struggling to accept myself,' she admitted through stuttering gulps of breath.

'I know we haven't got off to the best start, but I'm being honest when I say I want to help speed your recovery as much as I can.'

It was true. This mission might have started as a favour to her mother but Ed genuinely wanted to help Georgiana. He knew the hardship involved for those with mobility issues. His brother Jamie's fight had affected the whole family. That was why he did what he did here. To give every patient, every family, the chance to reach their full potential.

The clinic could give her a boost physically and, given tonight's outburst, she needed a friend to get her through this. Though he was sure she'd never say as much. Her pride and obstinacy had got her this far but there was a chance it could prevent her progressing any further. He recognised something of himself in her. That determination to do everything herself was in line with the responsibilities he shouldered with his family. It was better for him to be on his own dealing with everything than put the burden on anyone else's shoulders.

Perhaps that was why she'd been on his mind since their fraught first meeting. He'd watched her work out to the point of exhaustion, sweat trickling down the back of her neck. Yet she'd carried on because she knew that was what it would take to meet her eventual goal. He was a hypocrite for warning her about burning herself out when he'd have acted exactly the same way.

Not many would've managed his workload, balancing a successful, demanding career while caring for his loved ones. He did because he saw no other choice. At least, not one he cared to entertain. Like Georgiana, he didn't want strangers getting involved and taking over his duties. He managed and though committing his time to her too was going to put further strain on him, he'd do it. Because she needed him. He'd never turn down someone in trouble when he had the capacity to help and potentially change her life for the better with his work here.

Anything else that drew him to her— those troubled brown-green eyes, her fierce spirit and her blatant disregard for anything he said—were extraneous. Yes, the quicker they were able to get Georgiana to the level of fitness and recovery she was happy with, the better. Then he had no need to see her again or keep her on his list of people to care about.

Georgiana didn't know how long they'd been sitting on the wet floor but it was the most comforted she'd been since her operation. It was probably the only time she'd let anyone hold her, much less see her cry. She didn't know why he was different. Perhaps it was simply because he was there when she was at her lowest or that he didn't shy away from her when she barked at him. Most likely it was because on some level he seemed to understand what she was going through. He wasn't pushing her to talk the way everyone else did.

She supposed he'd seen a lot of people in her situation and she wasn't anything special to him. Yet he was here, pretending this was perfectly normal behaviour. Not for her it wasn't and, regardless of his poolside manner, she knew she'd come to regret this whole scene. This was the opposite of surviving on her own.

'I should get changed. I've taken up way too much of your time. I'm sure you have someone waiting up for you at home, cursing me up and down.' As soon as she withdrew from his body heat she began to shiver uncontrollably.

'I'll grab your things for you. You can change where you're sitting. I promise I won't look.' He was joking around with her, easing the intensity of the situation. It didn't escape her attention that he'd avoided confirming or denying if he had anyone to go home to.

Edward collected some extra towels, her clothes and, to her horror, her prosthetic. Technically it counted as one of her 'things' and he wouldn't think anything of it, but she'd never get used to treating it as casually as any other accessory.

'Thanks.' She took the pile from him and set it beside her, her leg balancing on the top.

True to his word, Edward turned away and put some distance between them. The changing room wasn't far but getting there would've been another humiliation too far.

'We should arrange a proper timetable so we know where we both stand. If you let me know what nights you want to come, I can make the arrangements.' He kept talking as he walked, preventing any awkward silence as she dried and attached her leg.

'I was thinking of coming most nights if that's possible? I know that's asking a lot of you.'

'No. That's fine. Same time? Same exit strategy?' Georgiana could hear the smile in his voice and was glad he was comfortable enough to make fun of her. So many tiptoed around her it was insulting. She'd lost a limb, not her sense of humour or any IQ points.

'As long as you remember to bring your invisibility cloak for me. Oh, you might want to pop a mattress in the back of the car too.' She only realised how that sounded as she pulled her top on.

'Excuse me? I know things have thawed between us but I'm not that kind of guy.' A shocked Edward was peering back at her when she popped her head through her hoodie.

She was certain he was exactly that kind of guy but she was horrified her jokey remark could be construed as some sort of sleazy come-on.

'I didn't mean… I was talking about for in here in case I fell again.' The end of this night couldn't come a second too soon. At this point in time she just wanted to get into bed, pull the covers over her and forget how big a fool she'd repeatedly made of herself tonight.

Silence. Then to her relief he laughed, a deep hearty chuckle that echoed around the room and caught her in the midst of its warm embrace.

'Edward!' she scolded but she was relieved he was teasing her rather than offended by her unintentional advances.

'Ed, please. Edward's so formal. Only business acquaintances give me the full first-name treatment.' He came over and stretched out a hand to help her up to a standing position. Usually she would refuse, to make a point, but they were past that now. She accepted his hand graciously.

'Thank you, Ed.'

'Does this mean I can call you Georgie now?'

'Definitely not.'

He insisted on taking her to his office, stopping to retrieve an ice pack on the way. Georgiana couldn't believe the sight she was greeted with on opening the office door.

'Excuse the mess. I'm working on something.' Ed made an attempt to tidy away the papers littering his desk and the floor but she'd seen enough for the guilt to surface.

'You should've said you were swamped with paperwork. I'd never have dreamed of taking you away from work if I'd known.' Not that she'd given him a chance to explain he didn't have time to entertain her tonight. Looking back, she'd dictated what he was doing and at what time. Perhaps she'd inherited a smidgen of that self-centred streak from her parents after all.

'It's fine. Take a seat. It's just a charity idea I'm working on. Nothing that can't wait.' He pulled a chair over for her and placed the ice pack gently on the back of her head where she'd hit the floor.

Georgiana flinched as the cold compress met the tender area on her scalp. 'What's the charity? Is this something the clinic is championing?'

'No, it's a personal venture of mine. A children's charity for young amputees. New limbs aren't dished out as and when they're needed. There's a budget, a limit on what these kids can have. Generally, that means nothing fancy and it certainly doesn't cover sports blades or water limbs. The government, much the same as my business partner, tends to deal in figures rather than human stories.' He handed her a sheaf of papers with the smiling faces of children beaming out from the stark white sheets of A4.

'These are patients of yours?'

'Some. Others are possible candidates who could benefit from the scheme. Not everyone can afford private healthcare, but I want this available to all. If we can get the funding. I have a list of potential donors but I'm having trouble finding somewhere willing to host a gala dinner where I can present my ideas and secure some business sponsors. Not everyone wants to support a worthy cause if they're not making money from it themselves.'

Georgiana watched disappointment gradually cloud the absolute joy that had been on Ed's face when he was talking about the subject. It seemed such a shame for the whole thing to stall at the start line when such a great idea could do so much good. She'd seriously underestimated this man and his good intentions. It put her to shame when she was in a position of some influence and chose to hide rather than help the less fortunate as Ed was doing. Although she wasn't ready to put herself out there personally, there was something she could do to contribute and to pay him back for his generosity and compassion towards her. It apparently hadn't crossed his mind to ask her for help or even advice on the subject.

'Why don't I ask my parents if you could host the event at the palace? I'm sure they'd be happy to contribute in some way even if it is just to donate the use of the ballroom for one night.'

'Do you think so? That would be amaz-

for health and safety violations. Although, he doubted she'd want anyone to know about her tumble when she was embarrassed enough that he'd been there to witness it.

In a way he was glad he had been there, not only to help her, but to provide the emotional support she so clearly needed too.

Besides, it wasn't Georgiana's fault he was so tired today. What was supposed to have been a brief stop at his parents' house had gone on longer than expected when he'd discovered some loose carpeting at the top of their stairs. He wouldn't have slept at all for worrying if he hadn't taken the time to nail it back in place. If either of them had tripped and fallen he'd never have forgiven himself.

Giles slurped his coffee and Ed was sure he was doing it only to make him jealous. He wasn't the kind of person to make enough for anyone else who might be in dire need.

'It's just that you've been mainlining caffeine since you got here and I'm sure you're wearing the same clothes you had on last night.'

'I'm not but thank you for caring. Late one at my parents' last night.' He was spending more time over at theirs doing little jobs to make sure they were safe. They seemed oblivious to the dangers around them now they weren't as fit or spry as they used to be, but he was the only one who really visited or ran their errands for them. At the end of the day they were his family and he didn't begrudge giving them a helping hand. Though some extra sleep would be nice.

'No problems with your visitor, then?' Giles was doing his best to keep the conversation casual but his continual hovering in the doorway spoke of his concern. Ed wasn't going to jeopardise Georgiana's nights here by confirming there'd been any sort of a problem. They'd had a small incident but he'd take steps to ensure it would never happen again. He wouldn't want her to end up in that situation a second time.

'Nope. Ms Ashley did her workout and I took her home afterwards. Nothing to report.' He couldn't quite meet Giles's eyes but it was only a white lie to save Georgiana's blushes. It had been nice having someone to confide in about his plans for the charity and she was doing him a huge favour in possibly securing a room at the palace for the event. If everything went to plan he'd have a venue for the gala dinner and an exclusive one at that. He couldn't see anyone turning down an invitation to the palace. Including Giles.

'Good, but if you're planning on doing the

same this evening you might want to try and wake yourself up a bit. Bags under the eyes don't make a good impression.' Ed couldn't blame him for wanting to cover the clinic's back as well as his concern for his workload. In the past Giles had suggested getting his parents into some sort of community housing to ease his burden but Ed wouldn't hear of it as long as he was able to keep them in their own home. The family home he'd grown up in with his brothers and sisters.

'If you were that bothered you would've brought an extra cup of coffee with you.' Ed crumpled up a piece of paper and lobbed it in his direction. Giles dodged it, spilling only a drop of his precious liquid cargo.

'I thought I'd encourage you to move and make your own to wake you up.' Giles flapped his hand across the steam, wafting the aroma across the room, then walked away chuckling to himself.

Despite the teasing, Ed could see his point. He still had a few hours to put in before Georgiana's session, then he'd be calling in on his parents to see what they needed. This drowsy state he was in wasn't going to be conducive to the rest of his working day.

He gave himself a mental shake and got up

out of the chair he'd been too comfy in for most of the day.

'If the pool isn't busy, I'm going to jump in for a dip,' he informed Giles as he passed him in the corridor outside his office.

'Good man. All I ask is for you to remember to put on a pair of swim shorts. It's not adults-after-dark time just yet.'

'Ha-ha. Very funny.' It was unnerving to have Giles making jokes at his expense when it was usually the other way around. More than that, he was unused to this fizzing in his veins with the reminder he was going to see Georgiana again tonight. He couldn't remember acting this way around any visitors to the clinic before. As Giles had said, he'd had more caffeine than was good for him today. Perhaps he needed to detox.

It was such a different atmosphere around the pool in the afternoon compared to the evening. All business and work, despite the happy faces of patients and staff and constant chatter. The bright glare of fluorescent light felt intrusive when being here with Georgiana had given him a new perspective of the place. With only two of them under minimum lighting it had been intimate, no room for all these people here now.

She would've hated to have been surrounded by all this toing and froing and not only because she was hung up on her appearance. Ed knew she remained in denial about what had happened to her. It wasn't unusual for someone who'd had their life and possible future wiped away from them out of the blue. Being surrounded by other people at different stages of their recovery with their trainers would've been too much reality for her to deal with all at once. Yet Ed knew she needed support as much as every other person here. It was simply going to take a different approach to get her to accept that. She'd do much better with a one-to-one than being faced with anything more confrontational. He was picking her up in a few hours so he'd have to come up with something quick before then.

His recreational swim wasn't important compared to the therapies being offered to those using the facilities. Ed was happy to wait his turn at the edge of the pool watching his patients' progress. They all knew him to see and most waved or shouted over at him, unbothered by his presence.

Lots of people were happier to come here than the gym or the physio rooms so there was a positive vibe. Except for whatever commotion was going on in the corner of the pool closest to him.

'Look, Hannah, I'll come in with you. All you have to do is let go of Mummy.' Ellie, one of their young trainers, had immersed herself in the water, uniform and all, in an effort to get her little patient in with her.

'No!' Hannah crawled further up into her mother's embrace, clinging onto her neck like a baby monkey.

The exasperated parent tried to loosen the child's grip around her throat. 'Hannah, you're hurting Mummy now. Let go, please.'

The little girl was one of their new patients. He'd met her when she came in for her initial assessment after losing part of her leg in a car accident. Paediatric amputees were always difficult. It was an adjustment for the child as well as their parents and he could see the frustration on the mother's face when she wanted her daughter to make as much progress as she could.

'Is there anything I can do to help? Hi, Hannah, remember me? Ed?' He slid into the water where the trio were, Hannah still refusing to let the water touch any part of her. She shyly put her head on her mother's shoulder and began to suck her thumb.

'We're introducing her to hydrotherapy

today.' Ellie pinked as he interrupted the temper tantrum going on in the shallow end.

'She's not having any of it.' The exasperated mother tried again to prise her off. 'Look, Hannah, the doctor's here. Don't you want to show him what a big girl you are?'

'No!' She wriggled, struggling to get away from the attention on her.

'It's okay,' he mouthed to the mother. 'If she's not ready we're not going to force her.'

Hannah was finding life as an amputee challenging. As were her parents. She was resisting any attempts to get her fitted for a prosthetic leg so they could start helping her try to walk again. So far, she was content to get around under her own steam, shuffling about on her bottom and asserting her independence. Her behaviour wasn't unlike some other remarkable young woman he knew. It was the sign of a strong individual and he knew they simply had to find a new way to get through to her. He'd figure it out. It was too important to the child's future to simply let her slip from their grasp.

Ever since confirming tonight's session with Ed, Georgiana had had that fluttery, fidgety feeling spreading through her body. Other than sitting in with her mother taking lunch, keeping her company while her father was doing her share of royal duties, she hadn't been able to settle.

There had certainly been big changes in her life when an evening training session had her blood pumping. Once upon a time it had been the thought of going out on patrol into enemy territory that had had the same effect.

After the previous evening's events she no longer considered Ed and his clinic enemy territory. Now she could see the benefits, knew what was on offer, she was looking forward to revisiting. She could do without a replay of her damsel-in-distress routine and jump-starting Ed's instinct to protect her. It wasn't in keeping with their usual dynamic where he let her make her own decisions and mistakes without judgement.

Of all the people around her and despite his profession, he was the one she hated to think of her as helpless. Until last night he'd treated her as an equal, as able-bodied, regardless of appearances to the contrary. The worst thing about it all for Georgiana was that she'd found it cathartic weeping into his chest as though she were some delicate flower. For a short while he'd allowed her to let the strong façade slip and be honest with her emotions.

She'd wanted to cry for a long time, to

cling to someone who would stroke her hair and let her fall apart in their arms without embarrassment on either side. Now she'd done it and got it all out of her system, she felt cleansed and almost back to her old self. It had been a moment of weakness. Clearly, she'd gone soft since leaving the army.

Tonight, they'd employed the same tactics as last night to smuggle her out. Goodness knew what the staff thought he was doing here, visiting for only a few minutes at a time, but she wasn't about to stop simply to put an end to any potential murmurings.

Ed had left her alone tonight to complete her workout but she was under strict instructions to find him if she fancied a swim.

Her muscles were crying out for relief and she'd thought ahead to pack a swimsuit this time. It didn't prevent her from hovering outside his door, uncertain if she should go ahead and knock.

In the end, the lure of the chlorine was too tempting to resist. She rapped on the office door. Instead of giving a reply, Ed yanked the door open. He'd been waiting for her.

'Georgiana? Are you ready to leave already?'

It was the shock that left her at a loss for

words, not the sight of him with his shirt undone and sleeves rolled up his thick, tanned forearms. She should be used to his casual dress outside professional working hours but it seemed to surprise her every time.

'No. I...uh...not yet. I thought I might go for a swim first, but if you're busy with your charity project I can leave it for tonight.'

'I could probably do with shutting off for a while. I've been trying to find a guest speaker for the gala. Someone to give us some prestige and help drum up some interest in sponsors.'

'Um...hello. Princess here.' It was infuriating, not to mention insulting, that he didn't ask her for help, which he clearly needed. He was the first person she seemed to turn to these days.

'Really? You'd be okay with speaking at the event? I wasn't sure you'd be comfortable enough yet with appearing in public.'

'I'm going to have to do it at some point. It's part of the job description. Besides, it's for a good cause and I can relate better to the kids you want to help than some reality-TV star.'

'Absolutely. As long as it's not going to be too much for you, that would be absolutely amazing.' Ed looked visibly lighter, not to mention astounded that she was willing to bail him out. She wondered why it was such a surprise that someone would want to reciprocate the kindness he showed towards people every day.

'I'm hoping by the time it comes around I'll be ready to go back into the land of the living,' she joked, but she was already freaking out about what she'd agreed to do. It had been a knee-jerk reaction to knowing he needed assistance and wanting to ease his workload. Like her, he was someone who obviously didn't depend too much on others to get the job done. He was beginning to show her how counterproductive that was at times. Sometimes more could be achieved by accepting a hand every now and then.

'We'll do our best to make that a possibility. Now I can go and have that swim with one less worry on my mind. I'll get ready and meet you outside the changing rooms. Try not to break anything until I get there.' It wasn't the charming smile that was devastating her as much as the words accompanying it.

'You're going in the pool too?'

'Yeah. I did say you'd need someone with you.' He looked concerned that she was querying his decision, when she hadn't considered he would actually be getting in the pool with her.

'But I thought…' She didn't know what she'd thought. It would've been creepy if he'd told her he'd be keeping an eye on her via CCTV. With all her demands for privacy he couldn't very well have drafted someone else in to do the job either. She hadn't really left him with any options since she'd shown him she couldn't be trusted on her own.

He was waiting, listening for her version of their crossed wires, but she wouldn't make a big deal of it. After all, it surely would've been more uncomfortable for both of them if he'd had to sit fully clothed at the side of the pool watching her. 'It doesn't matter. Just don't get in my way.'

'Yes, ma'am.' He gave her a mock salute, at which she didn't even pretend to hide her non-impressed face.

Georgiana was torn between leaving the changing room at all and ignoring his instruction to wait, jumping straight in the pool. There were numerous difficult decisions she had to make on a daily basis now. Such as whether to take her leg off now or poolside.

It was a toss-up between losing her dignity by having to hop across the floor and potentially risk another floor show or removing it in front of him. In the end she opted for walking out with a modicum of dignity. Ed wouldn't consider removing a prosthetic leg to swim anything out of the ordinary in his line of work. She had to keep telling herself that.

'Don't worry, I'm not going to get my stopwatch out.' He was waiting for her as promised outside the changing room. Georgiana would confess to being somewhat distracted by his physical appearance now that he was bare-chested and she could see exactly what he'd been hiding under those restrictive shirts.

Broad and toned just as she'd known he would be. With a smattering of golden-brown hair on his chest, which became darker as it trailed down his torso and disappeared into his blue swim shorts.

'Pardon me?' It was hypocritical of her to be staring at his body, appreciating it from a merely aesthetic point of view when it was the thing she was most afraid of herself. Although her fairly plain black all-in-one was more than he had seen her in lately.

'I mean I'm not assessing your form or treating this as some sort of training session. I'm here strictly to prevent you from hurting yourself again.' He was teasing her. She was getting used to seeing that light in his eye and tilt of his mouth as he baited her. Now she recognised it as the good humour he intended it to be, she didn't rise to it.

'You know you could do that from a distance, fully dressed, right?' In keeping with their new dynamic, she threw a dismissive glance at his swimwear this time. Ed wasn't liable to take offence. He was much too sure of himself to be self-conscious wearing a non-revealing pair of shorts. Budgie-smuggler trunks might have been a very different story for both of them.

'I thought I'd mix business with pleasure.' He gave her a wink and pulled on a pair of swimming goggles. Georgiana was left wondering which category she fell into as he dived into the water, his body a perfect arch as he hit the surface.

With Ed doing the front crawl away from her, she could take her time getting pool ready knowing she wasn't under surveillance. She wasn't quite as impressive hitting the water but it sure felt good to take the pressure off her limbs.

Ed was already on his second lap by the time she reached the deep end but she didn't care. This wasn't a race or somewhere she had to prove she was every bit as good as her previously able-bodied self. She saw this as more of a wind-down, therapy for the mind rather than her body.

She rested her arms on the edge of the pool, kicking her leg out in front of her to keep afloat as she watched Ed's progress. His fitness levels and confidence were evident in every stroke. The pace was more than she could manage now but, as he'd said, it wasn't a competition. She shouldn't envy the ease with which he covered the length of the pool.

Ed popped his head up beside her, removed his goggles and rested his elbows back on the edge of the pool.

'Can I ask you a question?' He rubbed one hand over his head, raking his hair into wet spikes.

'Sure.' As long as it wasn't anything personal. She was becoming more comfortable in his company now he'd seen her at her worst and hadn't run off screaming. It was nice to be around someone who treated her normally. The only thing that could ruin that would be having to talk over any serious, painful personal stuff about her family or what had happened to her.

'You do seem to enjoy the water. How helpful did you find aqua therapy during your recovery period? I mean, I know we use it here, but, personally, did it help you?'

Georgiana could tell his question arose from genuine curiosity rather than simply prying into her private life. It made it easier to answer.

'Yes, but possibly not in the way you'd imagine.' Judging by the raised eyebrows, she decided he wasn't expecting that response.

'Oh? Didn't you find it useful exercise during rehabilitation? I assume they did have hydrotherapy pools at the clinic where you had your after care?'

'Sure. The strengthening exercises were less painful in the water compared to the gym because of the hydrostatic pressure. It's known to improve respiratory function without overtaxing the body.'

'But?'

So far, she got the impression she was telling him something he already knew, since it was part of their programme for their amputee patients.

'It's more about the mindset of being in the water, if that makes sense… When I'm on solid ground the onus is very much on walking or doing everything on two legs, which is no longer natural for me. It's different in the water. I can almost forget I'm not normal now. I no longer need the leg or hoist to swim, float or splash around. You know, have fun.' She flicked her fingers across the surface of the water, spraying Ed, who didn't seem to mind in the slightest.

'It's good to know for future patients that even if they can't manage the exercises or prosthetics, they can still get something out of this.' He was pensive, as if he already had someone in mind, and Georgiana was curious about this person who'd grabbed his attention.

'Glad to be of help. Is this a hypothetical fishing expedition or are you thinking about someone in particular?' It was ludicrous for her to dig for more info as though she were a jealous girlfriend or a patient with a crush. Strictly speaking she wasn't a patient and he probably had some sort of gagging order preventing him from talking about people he treated. It was none of her business and she really didn't know why she was getting all worked up about the idea he could be swimming after hours with another secret visitor.

'A little girl who's having some trouble adapting. Hannah.'

Relief whooshed through her, chasing away her irrational territorial hold of Ed at the thought of sharing her swimming partner. She wanted to give herself a good slap for being so stupid about the whole matter.

'How so?'

A smile played across his lips as he thought about her question. 'She doesn't like being told what to do. Reminds me of someone, but I can't imagine who.'

'Ha-ha. Some of us simply know our own minds. It could be you simply don't know how to deal with a strong independent woman.'

Ed laughed. 'She's four years old but you could be right. Hannah's refusing to wear a prosthetic or go anywhere near the water.'

'And your usual charm offensive isn't working?'

'I know you'll find this hard to believe but, no, it isn't. I must be losing my mojo.'

Georgiana liked that he wasn't afraid to make fun of himself, even if he was frustrated by another patient refusing to fall in line with his usual tried and tested ways.

'Oh, I doubt that. You just have to find a new way of getting her to trust you. She's not going to co-operate until she sees what's in it for her. Everything about life after an amputation is a difficult journey. Even more so at that age, I'd say. She's not going to put herself through any more pain if she can't see the benefit of it. Take me as an example. I didn't want a part of you or this clinic. I had no reason to believe you had anything to offer me of any benefit. Yet, the promise of a swimming pool and some privacy and I'm hiding on the back seat of your car.'

In the end she'd wondered what he'd got out of the arrangement but after seeing him here in a quandary over a little girl, she knew. The satisfaction of knowing he'd done everything in his power to help. Georgiana was grateful for his perseverance and she knew Hannah's parents would feel the same about his personal attention.

'I'm not sure that would be appropriate in these circumstances.' He twisted his body around in the water so he had his back to the wall beside her, kicking his legs out in front. From a distance they would've looked like any other two swimmers taking a rest and having a chat. That was all Georgiana wanted. To be unremarkable.

'You're going to have to work hard to get on her good side, the way you did with me.' Georgiana was becoming increasingly involved in the story, since she knew what a difference it was having her prosthesis. If the child was to experience everything life had to offer it would be in her best interests to take advantage of everything being offered to aid her recovery.

'I'm on your good side? Good to know.' He looked pleased with himself at that snippet of information. Georgiana immediately had the urge to wipe the smirk off his face, lest he think he had won her over so easily.

'For now.' She pushed herself away from the side of the pool, accidentally on purpose splashing him as she kicked out.

'Oh, you're in for it now!' Ed shouted after her, spurring her pace. That sudden competitive edge between them made her heart race that little bit faster too.

The water swirled and moved alongside her as he launched himself after her. Georgiana went to give an excitable shriek, only to inhale a mouthful of water. It went up her nose and down her throat, making her choke. Panic swamped her and she dipped under the water. She lost focus, tried to get herself upright, forgetting she no longer had two feet to steady herself on the bottom of the pool. Now she was gulping the water, splashing desperately in an attempt to keep herself afloat.

Arms caught around her waist, pulling her from the depths, hands holding her fast until she broke the surface and could breathe again.

'I've got you. Just anchor yourself to my waist and take slow, deep breaths.' Ed's face was so close to hers she had nowhere to look but into his eyes, his mouth issuing instructions she was compelled to follow.

She wrapped her arms around his neck, her leg around his middle, which she wouldn't have done in any other circumstances save for the immediate threat of drowning.

She was relying on him saving her, letting him feel her disability for himself. Yet he was calming her, taking her mind off everything that frightened her by maintaining eye contact and syncing her breathing to his. Deep breaths in and out. Until the panic subsided and they were left entwined, her chest heaving against his, their breath mingling, eyes locked. They'd moved on from potential drowning incident to...well, she didn't know what.

Eventually Ed spoke. His voice hoarse as though he were the one who'd inhaled half of the pool. 'Are you okay?'

She wanted to say no, she wasn't okay with any of this. Either proving him right that she couldn't be left alone in here or about this overwhelming urge to kiss him. She didn't know where that thought had sprung from other than their sudden physical proximity.

Yes, he was single as far as she knew. Why wouldn't a woman want to snog the face off him? It was the knowledge that she wasn't necessarily someone he'd want to kiss back that stopped her. At least, not any more.

'Yes. Thanks. I lost track for a moment and panicked. Sorry. I'm all right now.' She attempted to extricate herself from him but he held her fast.

'You've had a fright. Let me—' He started to tread water with her still attached.

'No. I said I'm fine. I'm not an invalid.' With that she shoved hard against his chest so he let go, then swam away. This time she was very well aware of her inadequacies. She'd had them wrapped around Ed's waist.

CHAPTER FIVE

ED TOOK HIS time showering and changing, trying to get his head around what had nearly happened. When Georgiana had begun play-fighting, showing him a fun side he hadn't seen before, all he'd wanted to do was encourage it and indulge his own. It seemed a lifetime since he'd really cut loose from work and his home life and let himself be free.

That burst of spontaneity hadn't come without cost. Both he and Georgiana had put her in danger with their game of one-upmanship. Their lack of judgement nearly causing a catastrophe.

When she'd started floundering he'd cursed himself for putting her in that position. It had left her vulnerable and made him think of the time when she'd been hurt. Her pain, her strength, her courage and subsequent fight to live.

Ed grabbed a towel and dropped it over his

head, shutting out the world and leaving him in the dark with his jumbled emotions. What bothered him most about the incident in the pool was the aftermath. When the danger had passed and he and Georgiana were left entwined in the water. He hadn't wanted to let her go. For a brief second he'd thought he'd seen the same hesitation in her eyes.

Something had flared to life between them and he knew it was more than a primitive reaction to holding a beautiful woman so close. He'd wanted to kiss her, and not just some patronising peck on the lips to assure her she was still alive and breathing. Ed had wanted to taste the sweetness and passion of the woman who'd been constantly on his mind since they'd met and drink her in. Until he was the one drowning.

A sharp rap on the changing room door dragged him out of his thoughts.

'Are you still alive in there?' It was Georgiana checking on him, letting him know he'd been lost in his reverie for too long.

'Give me a minute.' He dressed in double-quick time, his hair and skin still damp.

She was leaning against the wall outside when he finally managed to gather his things. He felt guilty about keeping her waiting but at least she'd hung around. Given her reaction to

him in the pool, he wouldn't have been surprised if she'd made her own way back home.
Perhaps she had no one to call for a lift or no
money for a taxi.

He hoped she'd forgiven him for the pred-
atory way he'd surely been looking at her so
they could put it behind them. After all, it
hadn't meant anything. It couldn't.

'You took your time. I thought you were
suffering from delayed shock in there.'

He had in a way.

'No. Just shaving my legs,' he deadpanned
and shut the conversation down.

As they stepped out into the autumnal air, Ed
was dreading the thought of taking Georgiana home and then going on to his parents'
house. Despite the complications, their time
in the pool had given him a sense of release.
A freedom he wasn't yet ready to surrender.

'Would you like to go for a coffee? There's
a place down the road that should still be
open.' What was more normal than having
a chat over a cuppa? Making small talk in a
public area should help erase whatever had
almost happened between them.

'Er…' Her eyes darted everywhere but at
him. She gave the impression she was un-

comfortable at the thought but didn't know how to break it to him.

Ed wasn't the sort of man who refused to take no for an answer. He'd bow out gracefully with what was left of his pride.

'It's not a problem. You want to get home. I understand.' He pulled down the shutter on the door and locked it tight, not wanting to prolong Georgiana's agony any longer than necessary if she wanted rid of him.

'It's not that. We've gone to so much trouble to keep my identity hidden on these visits it seems reckless to stroll into a coffee shop now.'

'Of course. Sorry.' He slapped his hand to his head. 'I'd completely forgotten you're supposed to be incognito.'

He'd stopped thinking of her as a princess or someone he was doing a favour to. Which should've been insulting to a member of the royal family, to completely disregard her heritage or status, but Georgiana seemed delighted.

'Really?'

He took a good look at her. Free from the heavy kohl eye make-up she favoured and her hair soft, no longer spiky with product, she was simply a beautiful young woman to him.

'Really.'

'The truth is I'd love to do something as ordinary as order a latte and a pastry, but I could do without the circus which would inevitably follow if I was recognised.'

'Get over yourself, Georgiana. You look as much like a princess right now as I do.' He swept his hair back with a toss of his hand and made her laugh, the sound so moreish he wanted to make her do it again and again.

She stuck her tongue out at him, then plonked her trusty baseball cap on her head. 'You know, I do have an adrenaline buzz going on. I suspect it's something to do with nearly drowning.'

'You were never in any real danger. Although I might advise you to wear a life jacket for any future pool shenanigans.' He was glad they were back to their vocal jousting best, any awkwardness consigned to the past. It meant he no longer had to obsess over what had happened or how he'd felt when he'd held her.

'Or perhaps a lifeguard who does evening shifts?'

A surge of something bitter swelled in the pit of his stomach as she floated the idea of another man taking over their secret swim sessions. He didn't like it.

'About that coffee…you might have to

change your order to something decaffein-ated. Perhaps a milky drink like a hot choc-olate to help you sleep later.' To his surprise she linked her arm through his as they walked down the street.

'What? I thought it would look less suspi-cious if we pretend we're together instead of walking in separately.'

'Not because you want me to pay?'

'Hey, you were the one who asked me out.'

'There's a seat in the corner by the door. Try not to be too princessy until I get back.' He directed her towards a small table for two crammed into the corner of the café.

Georgiana chose to sit with her back to the rest of the shop to maintain a low profile, but it went against all her army training. She couldn't see who was coming in or might be behind her. Blind to anyone who could ap-proach. She'd have to rely on Ed for surveil-lance as well as security. He wouldn't mind and, strangely, neither did she.

Over these past days he'd proved she could trust him with her life and her secrets. Loy-alty was highly prized now that her privacy meant everything.

'One milky, adrenaline-free hot chocolate with extra cream and marshmallows for you and one for me.' A tall glass mug layered with sugary goodness appeared in front of her and she inhaled the comforting aroma.

'All calorie free too, I assume?'

Ed tilted his head to one side. 'I don't think you need to worry yourself on that score.'

There was something in his lowered tone that zapped her right in the danger zone and made her blush. He'd seen most of her, felt most of her pressed up against him, and the reminder made her burn with more than embarrassment. She didn't think he was teasing her. He was missing the twinkle and the smirk she'd got used to when he was doing so. This time she swore his eyes had darkened and his voice got huskier, which only made her hotter.

That moment they'd had in the pool had sent her hurtling away from him for this very reason. These sudden urges towards him scared her. She didn't want to face what it meant when her life was already so complicated.

After her operation, she hadn't dared imagine having feelings for anyone again. Much less someone to be interested in her that way. Ed might tease her but he would never do anything ungentlemanly. Unless she asked him to.

'Two cheese and ham toasties.' The barista-cum-food-warmer set two plates down, disturbing the tense mood around the table.

'I didn't order anything,' she whispered to Ed, afraid of upsetting the member of staff and causing a scene.

'I know it's not your usual haute cuisine, Princess, but I thought you might be hungry after your swim.' Ed unfurled his cutlery from its paper envelope and sawed through his hot toasted sandwich.

Georgiana wasn't sure if hot chocolate and toasties were a food combination she totally approved of but her rumbling tummy made the decision for her.

'I am. Thank you.' It wasn't the best meal she'd ever eaten but the sentiment and company made the evening better than any she'd ever had in even a five-star establishment.

While she delicately cut her sandwich into bite-sized pieces, Ed attacked his with gusto. She noted his large hands, his eager mouth, and had to look away again. Horrified by the hormonal mess she'd become around him lately.

She chewed and swallowed her food but no longer tasted it. At this point she thought it might have been a better idea to have gone home when she'd had the chance.

Ed Lawrence was the wrong man for her on all sorts of levels. Probably. She was just having trouble remembering what those reasons were right now.

After taking a healthy mouthful of his hot chocolate, he'd coated his top lip with cream and melted marshmallow. She was mesmerised by the tongue licking it off and savouring the taste.

Goodness, they must've put the heating on in here because her temperature was spiking.

'Did you get a chance to ask your folks about hosting the gala at the palace?'

'Yes, they agreed. Sorry, I meant to let you know.' Georgiana was keen to have something other than Ed's eating habits and her own libido on her mind.

'That's such a weight off my mind. Thank you. I can hopefully set a date and send out the invitations now. This is actually happening.' He smiled as he shook his head as though he couldn't quite believe it. Despite all the hard work he'd obviously been doing to bring it to fruition.

'Yes, it is. Thanks to you.'

'And you. I thought I'd come to the end of the road. You saved us.'

'My parents aren't going to be present, of course. That's not part of the deal.' She shook off his undeserved praise. It was Ed who'd put his heart and soul, not to mention the extra hours of work, into setting this up.

'Understood.'

'Although, Mother does want to do her bit by bringing in her own caterers and florists for the occasion.' She'd been surprisingly keen to get involved when Georgiana had put the proposal to her. The cynic in her wondered if it was in some way to ease her conscience over her own amputee daughter.

'That's very generous of them.'

'Yeah. To their credit, my parents haven't been pushing me to go back to work yet. Speaking at the gala gives me something to work towards. It will be a test. I'm just holding out for that day when I, and the rest of the world, no longer care about my appearance.'

'I understand you have hang-ups about your prosthetic. It's a big change for you, but you lost a leg, not your life. What kind of existence are you going to have if you stay locked away from the rest of the world?'

'A quiet one,' she muttered, every inch the petulant child.

'That's what you want? I don't believe someone who has travelled the world and been in life or death situations could be content to rot away behind four walls. What would make you happy, Georgiana?'

'You don't understand. It's not about being happy or content. It's about not feeling any worse.' Someone who looked like an Aussie surfer and ran a successful business would never have her worries.

'So, tell me.' He sat back in his chair, arms folded, waiting for her to unload.

'I joined the army to get away from people staring and talking about me as though I'm not a real person.'

'That's the reason you went into service?' He raised an eyebrow in disbelief at her. She really wasn't explaining herself very well but it was the first time she'd tried to put how she was feeling into actual words.

'Not entirely. I wanted to be someone of worth, to do something I could be proud of and help people where I could.'

'You mightn't be able to go back to that now, but that doesn't mean you can't be an asset elsewhere. You're certainly going to be inspirational for my charity families.'

'I'm sure I'll make a great pin-up girl,' she scoffed.

'I never had you pinned as someone who sat around feeling sorry for herself.' Blotches of red blossomed in his cheeks but it was

Georgiana who felt the sting. Was that how he saw her? A spoilt rich girl feeling sorry for herself? After some thought she realised it wasn't an unreasonable conclusion to come to, given her recent behaviour.

'If you have parents who are more interested in public perception than the welfare of their children, you might realise why I'm so fixated on my...imperfection. As far as my mother's concerned, I'm damaged goods. The only way I could ever be right again is if I grew my leg back.' She thought of Freddie, her beautiful fun-loving brother. His perceived imperfection had been his sexuality. Something else to shame their parents.

Just as she couldn't change her circumstances, neither could Freddie. He hadn't been able to live with the disappointment any better than she could. Georgiana's way of coping was to hide away. Surely that was a better option than taking one's life? Depending on who you asked, of course.

'Really? I didn't get that impression from talking to her. She came across as being very proud of you.'

Any form of praise for her parents always darkened her mood.

'I'm sure she managed to give you that impression for the duration of her appointment.

Saving face is part of her job description. The reality is somewhat different.' Her mother didn't seem as proud when she was giving her those sideways glances of despair any time Georgiana had her false leg on show. She certainly hadn't been loud and proud about her colourful son either.

'Who do you think suggested I called in on you that first night? She's worried about you but afraid to go anywhere near you and who can blame her? You're a hard person to crack, Georgiana Ashley.'

There was that unpleasant sinking in her stomach again. A sense of betrayal and confusion about what had been going on behind her back dragging her down into despair.

'Is—is that why she hired you? To break me down?' She'd thought their meeting and subsequent forays at the clinic had been a happy quirk of fate. Finding out it was something her mother had orchestrated made a mockery of her and the emotions she'd begun experiencing around Ed.

The odd food combination she'd had along with this nauseating bombshell made her want to vomit.

Ed let out a groan of frustration and scrubbed his hands over his head. 'She didn' hire me for you. Your mother brought me i

for a consultation on her back injury. All she asked where you were concerned was to have a chat and make sure you were all right. Everything that happened after that arose from circumstance and opportunity. It wasn't a set-up.'

'Is that what all this was about? Be nice to the poor amputee who's so desperate for company she'll do anything in return?'

'Of course not. I'm not that kind of man, Georgiana. If I was trying to butter you up don't you think I'd take you somewhere more upmarket?' Now Ed was the one all puffed up with indignation, his voice carrying farther than she appreciated.

'I couldn't say. It's not as if I know you.' She leaned across the table to continue the argument in private, hoping to persuade Ed to do the same so as not to draw any attention from bystanders.

He looked as though she'd helped herself to his food as well as hers. His pain so palpable she could nearly feel it.

'I thought we were getting along well.' The laid-back Ed she'd thought him to be was gone, to be replaced with someone prepared to stand against the disservice she was doing him. He got up, walked over to the bin and

deposited his rubbish in one short, sharp motion before returning to the table.

Georgiana considered what he'd had to say and the way he was reacting to the suggestion their interaction this far had been a convoluted plot by her mother. It was blatantly obvious how annoyed he was in his tone and his body language. Unless he was an award-winning actor, she'd really insulted him.

She was both relieved and remorseful, even if none of this managed to change her mind.

'If I got that wrong, I apologise.' She was stubborn and defensive but when she was wrong, she admitted it. Something she'd learned was important from parents who would never confess to making mistakes. Apologies and acknowledgement of wrong-doings were vital for closure. Poor Freddie never got his and she doubted she ever would either.

'You did get it wrong. Apology accepted.' The thin line of his mouth relaxed along with his frown. One good thing about a man who didn't sweat the small stuff was that he didn't appear to hold a grudge either. Georgiana wished she were more like him.

Whatever Ed might think, she didn't see what difference she could make to anyone's life when her own was so pathetic the one person who'd befriended her now stood accused of being paid off to do so.

How was such a paranoid, needy loser going to improve someone else's lot? Unless she was held up as an example of what not to become. None of this changed her mind about the situation.

Ed waved a white paper napkin in surrender. 'Truce?'

What choice did she have but to agree to a ceasefire in hostilities when he was the only person she had to talk to?

She took her time finishing her drink, knowing they were going to be locked in the car soon, where she'd be suffocated under that damned blanket and the reminder of failing her public duty.

The door to the coffee shop was thrown open and a young family burst in. Their excited chatter filled the air and took the pressure off her to try and make more conversation with Ed.

'What do you want, Ethan?' The young dad ushered his boisterous son into a booth next to them, followed by his other half, who was pushing a buggy.

'Hot chocolate.' The youngster climbed up on the back of the seat to stare over at Georgiana. She gave him a flash of a smile then pulled her baseball cap down again.

'Sit down, son, and leave the lady alone.' The father tugged him back down, making sure he was settled in a seat before he went to the counter.

The baby started wailing then to be released from its imprisonment, and as his mother was busy trying to pacify her youngest Ethan made a break for it again.

Georgiana couldn't see what was going on behind her but she could guess as draughts of cold air hit the back of her neck.

'Ethan, leave the door alone,' his father bellowed from the other side of the coffee shop.

'Time to go?' Ed suggested and Georgiana nodded her head enthusiastically. There'd been sufficient conflict for one night. She didn't need to be involved in anyone else's domestic.

'Yes, please.' She deposited her rubbish and they made their move to go.

Suddenly there was a blood-curdling scream drawing the attention of everyone in the café towards the door.

'Ethan!' The little boy's mother was screaming just as loudly as her son and it wasn't long before they saw why.

'He's trapped his fingers in the door.' Ed

hared off towards the sobbing boy, where the glass door was now smeared with tears and blood.

'We need a first-aid kit now. Now!' Georgiana shouted to the staff. She was straight back into medic mode faced with the emergency.

Ed held the door at an angle so she could ease the boy's hand out of the door jamb. Whatever he'd been up to, he'd managed to get his fingers caught inside the heavy hinged door.

The distraught parents rushed over but she knew it would be best for them to keep their distance until they managed to stem Ethan's injuries.

'We're both medical professionals. If you could phone an ambulance, we'll take care of your son.'

The dad immediately got out his mobile phone and the mum did her best to soothe both of their children while looking close to tears herself.

'It'll be okay, Ethan, baby.'

'They can't get anyone here for a while. All available ambulances have been diverted to a major emergency on the motorway.' Ethan's father relayed the bad news but Ed remained calm as he knelt down beside the boy. 'We'll take him to my clinic down the street. I can help him.'

He motioned Georgiana over and she could see why he was anxious to get the child to the clinic. The large gash running along the back of his hand was bleeding everywhere and so deep she could see exposed bone.

She grabbed a bottle of water from behind the counter, which Ed poured over the wound to clean it. Ethan yelled.

'Sorry, mate, we don't want anything nasty to get in there and cause an infection. Georgiana, can you get a dressing out for me?' Ed was holding the boy's hand up, trying to stem the flow of blood, and left it to her to inspect the contents of the first-aid kit provided by the staff.

She took out a wad of tissues and dabbed the area to dry it off before applying a sterile dressing. The wound was going to need stitching but that would keep it dry and clean until they could get him to the clinic. 'Are you doing okay, Ethan? Let me know if you start to feel sick or dizzy, okay?'

Shock was an important factor to look out for after any injury and particularly in one so traumatic, but Ethan's father gathered him up in his arms and Georgiana knew everyone was keeping a close eye on the boy to make sure he'd be okay.

They must have made an odd-looking procession as they made their way to the clinic premises. Ethan was still holding his hand up but the dressing was soaked with blood and the child was greyer than the overcast sky.

Ed was racing ahead to get the place opened. There was no way Georgiana could keep up with him without her gait giving away her secret. She stayed behind with the pram-pushing mum.

'Don't worry. Ed's a surgeon. He knows what he's doing.' There was no one better to have in a medical emergency.

The young woman nodded but didn't speak. As she was biting down hard on her lip, Georgiana could tell she was afraid of saying anything and breaking down when she was trying to be strong for her son. She had some inkling of what that was like.

'I'll wait out here to direct the paramedics. I'm not great with blood,' the mum finally admitted.

'You'll be better in the fresh air and it's probably not a bad idea to keep the baby out of it all.'

Georgiana managed to give her a reassuring pat on the back before disappearing inside after the others. They'd need as little distraction as possible in there.

Ed had set up in one of the treatment rooms, where bright lights were dazzling and Ethan was perched up on a bed with his arm stretched out.

'Georgiana, I'm going to need your help here.' Ed was sitting in a chair by the bed, carefully unwrapping the blood-soaked dressing from around the boy's hand.

'Okay.' His request caught her unawares as he seemed to have everything under control, but she was pleased he'd thought to include her. That her career history hadn't been completely consigned to the past along with having two good legs.

'If you could clean things up here again, I'm going to give him something for the pain.'

She sat on the bed beside Ethan, armed with the swabs and iodine Ed had provided.

'Hi, Ethan, my name is… Georgie.' It was important to her to draw a line somewhere between her public and private persona.

From the corner of her eye she could see Ed smirk, but this wasn't the time to get into one of their spats. She didn't have to explain her every move to him.

'We're going to get you cleaned up and give you something to take the pain away.'

'Ow!' he cried as she dabbed delicately at his hand.

'I know it hurts but this is all to make you better.'

Ethan buried his head into his dad's chest but let her do what she had to.

Ed turned back with a needle in his hand. 'You're going to feel a little scratch, Ethan, but this is going to take away the pain for you.'

Georgiana held the small hand in place for Ed to inject. It would make it easier to stitch and lessen the chance of infection setting in.

She had no doubt Ed could undertake that or any possible surgery should the need arise. He had that same temperament and skill that would've served him well if he'd chosen to work in a military environment.

'Good boy,' she encouraged when she saw Ethan tense at his advance.

Once the injection had been administered, Ed made sure the wound was clear and the area was numb before he began to suture.

'You'll feel a little tug when I'm stitching, Ethan, but it shouldn't be painful.' Ed pulled the sides of the skin together and closed them with the tiny needle and thread.

'It'll all be over in a second,' Georgiana soothed.

Once Ed had finished suturing, she applied another sterile dressing to cover the site and keep it clean and dry.

It was a revelation to her that she could still be of use in this field. Ed was the lead here but she knew she could've handled this on her own had it come to it. Her medical skills hadn't deserted her simply because her confidence had. What was more, this feeling of being useful in some capacity had given her spirits a lift. Which was more than any well-meaning words had managed from those around her.

She gave Ed credit for getting her to see she didn't have to resign herself to being on the scrap heap. Even if he'd been harsh in the delivery. Although they both knew she would never have responded to a soft approach.

If this feeling could be sustained, she wanted to capture it now. She could help, she could improve a child's life and she wanted to do it.

Ed gave aftercare instructions and told them to have the stitches taken out at the hospital, with a warning if there were any signs of infection to have Ethan's hand seen sooner. Georgiana waited until the family were on their way home before she approached Ed. Her blood was pumping in anticipation of discussing things with him. Positivity was surging in her veins, giving her a renewed sense of purpose. It was a small step but one in the right direction. One out of the shadows and into the light. Where hopefully a new future was waiting for her and others in her situation.

As they stood outside once more, the excitement over, Ed shut the clinic one final time. Georgiana inhaled a lungful of cool, clean air.

'I'd like to help with Hannah. I'll talk to her for you.' She didn't have time to consider the implications of another commitment she'd made as Ed grabbed her into a bear hug. It was good to be back in her rightful place.

CHAPTER SIX

ED HAD HELD his tongue the whole way back to the palace last night. Afraid to make a song and dance about Georgiana's decision in case she changed her mind in the cold light of day. After all they'd just been involved in a medical drama.

He was sure it had been a long time since she'd been involved in anything like that but Georgiana was on the phone first thing. Literally as soon as dawn broke.

'Hello?'

'Hello, Ed? This is Georgiana.' Her perky voice instantly made him sit upright in his bed so he didn't sound as though he'd been fast asleep only seconds before.

'What can I do for you?'

'I wanted to let you know I'm still available for that chat with Hannah if you can sort something out with her parents.'

'That's great. I'll call them when it's a

more reasonable hour.' He yawned, but waking up to the sound of her excitement wasn't the worst thing to start the day.

'Sorry for waking you. I haven't slept much.'

'It was a lot to deal with. I was going to call you anyway to see how you were after last night. You beat me to it.' She'd certainly been on his mind. Enough for Ed to wonder if he'd been dreaming when he'd heard her on the other end of the phone.

'Is it awful of me to say I got a real buzz out of it?'

'There's nothing like an emergency to get the heart pumping, is there? No need to feel bad about it. Ethan's going to be fine.'

'Now if we can do something for Hannah too…'

He liked the sound of 'we'. It denoted a bond as well as forgiveness for omitting to tell her from the start about her mother's involvement.

'Can I ask what prompted your decision to help?' He finally blurted out the question that had been on his lips since she'd mentioned it last night. She seemed in such good spirits and lacking that usual defensive attitude; he was curious about what had brought it about.

'It was Ethan actually. I'd forgotten what

it was like to be useful. I thought about what you said and you were right. My army days are behind me but I could have a new path waiting for me. It might take some adjusting but I want to do something other than being a burden to people. I want to make a difference.' Ed could hear the passion in her voice and it was intoxicating. Everything he'd wanted for her. Coming to terms with the end of her life as she'd known it was no small feat but after seeing her in action he knew she had so much more to give.

'I'm one hundred per cent behind you, Georgiana. You know that.' Ed was perched on the edge of his bed now.

'All I'm doing is talking to a little girl. One step at a time. Excuse the pun.' She was laughing at herself. Something else new and positive. Things Ed didn't want to be responsible for ruining.

'Thank you for agreeing to speak to Hannah. I know how much it took for you to agree to do that. I'll arrange a time with her parents and get back to you. Anything after that is totally in your hands, Georgiana.'

She wasn't someone who could be rushed into things. She moved at her own pace and made her own decisions.

Ed was hoping the clinic and he would be a part of any of her future plans.

Meeting a member of the public, no matter how young, brought all sorts of dilemmas for Georgiana. First of all, she'd had to decide if she wanted to make it an official engagement. Which would have entailed informing security, staff and making special arrangements at the clinic.

She'd gone for option B instead. The sneaking-out method.

There had also been the question of what to wear. It wasn't a diamonds and pearls event where she'd be expected to wear haute couture. No, this was worse. In order to get Hannah to relate to her she had to go with something to show off her prosthetic leg.

It was the thought of Ethan and the effusive thanks they'd received from his parents for helping that sealed her decision. She'd donned her usual casual gym kit that she was comfortable in.

Now she was waiting in Ed's office to be introduced to Hannah and her parents. As she paced the floor, her pulse was doing the samba, her skin was clammy and she wasn't altogether steady on her feet. Anyone would think she'd just run a marathon.

To keep herself busy she began to tidy the mess that was supposed to be Ed's desk. It was a curious insight into the man who'd put all this into motion. The dirty coffee cups lying around suggested someone too busy to be bothered with a trivial thing such as washing up at work.

What struck her most was the lack of personal touches in his workspace. There were no photos of family or items from home she'd expect to have crept into an environment where he spent most of his time.

She no longer thought of Ed as some beach bum who drifted through life. He was devoted to his job and patients if Hannah was any indication. With no obvious signs of his personal life, she wondered if this was because of his dedication to his career or something else. He knew a lot about her and she realised she wanted to find out more about Mr Lawrence beyond the job.

She heard voices in the corridor outside, saw the door handle move and her heart leapt into her throat. This wasn't a public event and as far as she knew there were no photographers around to capture the moment but she was just as anxious as though she were on the international stage.

Georgiana stood by the window, creating

a space between her and the people about to walk into the room.

'There's someone I'd like you to meet, Hannah.' Ed's voice filtered in first.

Georgiana took a deep breath.

Four more faces entered the room. One familiar and smiling, a little suspicious one and two open-mouthed and staring.

She swallowed down the anxiety threatening to choke her and moved forward with her hand outstretched. 'Hi, I'm Georgiana.'

The woman with the small child clinging to her like a koala was completely still, her gaze fixed on Georgiana.

Ed stepped forward to break the awkward moment of recognition. 'Georgiana, this is Hannah and her parents, Phil and Kate Howell.'

It was Phil who finally shook her hand. 'Pleased to meet you.'

'But you're, you're—' Kate's reaction to meeting a member of the royal family wasn't unusual but this was the first time Georgiana had faced it since her time in the army. She wasn't used to it any more.

Ed discreetly closed the door behind the family. 'Hannah, Georgiana is a princess and she has a poorly leg just like you.'

They'd discussed introductions before the

family arrived and she'd agreed that for once her royal status might prove helpful. By all accounts Hannah was obsessed with princesses and happy-ever-afters. Georgiana knew something about one of those things at least.

Although the little girl didn't seem convinced, her eyes narrowed and mouth pouting. 'She doesn't look like a princess.'

The words, though they'd come from a child, still struck her where it hurt most. Out of the mouths of babes, the truth was inescapable. Georgiana was a freak.

'Well, the princess is here to exercise. She wears her ball gowns and tiaras at home in the palace.' Ed was grinning at her and that urge to run and hide gradually died away.

Of course, she didn't look like a princess to a four-year-old who believed in fairy tales. In Hannah's head Georgiana should have long thick glossy hair, a perfect body and always be ready to accompany a handsome prince to a ball at the chime of the bells. She was the anti-princess. Ed, however, would've been perfect cast in the handsome prince role.

'Sorry, Hannah. This is how I am most days but I promise I do live in a palace.' It seemed absurd to be bragging about such a thing when she'd spent most of her life resenting it but, for once, this wasn't about her. When someone was in need, she would work with whatever she had in her kit to make them better. In this situation her heritage might prove more effective than a first-aid pack.

Hannah looked to her mum for guidance. 'Is she really a princess?'

Mrs Howell nodded. 'She really is.' Then she turned and whispered to Ed, 'Should we curtsey or something?'

'That's really not necessary. I'm just here to have a chat with Hannah. I hear you had a big operation the same as mine.' She saw the girl staring at her prosthetic and decided to bite the bullet. Pulling a chair over, she sat down and proceeded to remove her false leg.

Hannah's eyes widened as she removed the protective sock off the end of her stump. Georgiana couldn't bring herself to glance at Ed even though he'd seen her at her most vulnerable. Instead, she addressed the parents, who wouldn't have been aware of the circumstances leading to this.

'I'd appreciate it if you could keep this private. I'm still coming to terms with the injuries I sustained during my time in service and I'd prefer not to have the press hounding me during my recovery.'

'Of course.'

'We read about you joining the army but had no idea you'd been involved in active duty. Much less injured. I'm so sorry.'

It was daft but Mr and Mrs Howell's understanding and compassion made her well up. Usually any display of sympathy angered her, making her feel as though she was a figure to be pitied. Here, though, these people understood the implications and difficulties since they were going through the same with their daughter. They were the first *civilians* she'd shared this with and it was a hugely significant step for her. One that she wouldn't have taken without a push from Ed.

Seeing their honest, thoughtful reaction, she had a lot to thank him for. Perhaps her 'coming out' wouldn't be as bad as she'd feared.

'Why don't you take a seat?' Ed urged them forward and it was something of a relief to all be on the same level with no distinction between abilities or class.

Hannah was squirming in her mother's arms and making unhappy noises until she was set down on the floor. She shuffled on her bottom across the carpet towards Georgiana. Without saying a word she looked at her own stump, then at Georgiana's, comparing the two. She could obviously see the similarities despite the difference in size.

When Hannah reached out to touch her stump it was all she could do not to leap into the air. It didn't hurt, not any more, but that intimate recognition of how her body had changed remained a sore point.

She held her breath as the tiny hand explored the scarred tissue for what seemed an eternity.

'Hannah, you should have asked for permission first. I'm so sorry, Miss Ashley.' The girl's mother went to pull her back but Georgiana put a hand up to stop her.

'It's fine. She's curious, that's all.' There was no judgement being made, only a childish fascination she shouldn't take offence at.

Suddenly the little girl took hold of her hand and tugged it. Georgiana eased herself out of the chair so she could sit on the floor with her, their legs stretched out almost mirroring each other's.

Still holding Georgiana's hand, she placed it on her little stump where her leg used to be. The gesture took her by surprise. It was the connection everyone had been waiting for. A reminder that she wasn't alone. There were so many like her and Hannah, adults and children who needed support.

'Does it hurt?' she asked, when the scars and operation Georgiana had endured seemed too much for someone so young, so small, to have to deal with.

Hannah shook her head.

'You're not much of a talker, huh?' Georgiana didn't blame her for being uncooperative on so many different levels when so many strangers had come into her life uninvited recently. It was her way of keeping some control. The same reason Georgiana was clinging to her privacy.

'Only until she gets to know you, then she never shuts up.' Her father laughed and Hannah stuck out her tongue at him.

'Would you like to see my new leg?' Georgiana used her interest to their advantage and handed her prosthetic to Hannah for inspection. There was no doubt this was surreal, especially with an audience, to be waving about the leg she'd been trying so hard to hide.

Hannah had trouble lifting it off the ground and dragged it over to the end of her stump where it dwarfed her.

'This one's too big for you but I'll show you how it works.' She was sure to have seen videos and leaflets but perhaps it was different when confronted with the real thing. Hannah was playing with her trainer-clad foot, making it comically hop lopsided across the floor.

'We have some more your size, Hannah, if you want to see?' Ed had spotted the ideal opportunity to introduce her to the idea of prosthetics and fetched several samples for her to see.

'Hey! I never got to choose a colour.' Georgiana feigned outrage as the youngster was handed a hot-pink prosthetic. One surely fit for a princess or a lover of fairy tales.

'You should've come to me earlier,' Ed joked, but she'd been thinking the same thing herself. In the space of a few days in his company she was swimming again, treating medical emergencies and meeting people. If only she'd met him sooner her recovery might have been further on than it was currently. He pushed her to the limit without the sort of interference and control she'd feared. Whatever happened from here, she had a lot to thank him for.

This had been such a risk for Ed to take but worth it, judging by the smiles on everyone's faces. Hannah was full of wonder, handling and working out how the prosthetic moved. Her parents were sitting back, letting her explore without interference but seeming relieved. Then there was Georgiana. He hadn't seen her shine as brightly as she was now. Her eyes welling up with happy tears showing how much this meant to her too.

Hannah was responding to her, opening up to the idea of a prosthetic, and that could only bring positive news regarding her future. Georgiana was blossoming right alongside her. He was watching her interact, no longer self-conscious, and it was glorious.

'What's this funny one?' Hannah dumped one of the prosthetics in his lap, demanding his attention.

'This one is for running. It's called a blade. Do you see how it's curved at the bottom? It's springy too.' He bent down to demonstrate it, much to Hannah's amusement.

'There are all types of ones you can get and having one of these means you can walk on two legs again. Wouldn't you like to do that, Hannah?' Georgiana shifted back up into her seat and proceeded to attach her prosthesis.

Hannah was watching her every move with rapt fascination as her princess stood at full height. Mrs Howell gave a sob. This was such a milestone for them even Ed found himself getting choked up.

'I can make an appointment for you to get fitted for one of your own, Hannah.' He'd make sure to get her in as soon as possible before she changed her mind.

'Since you're here, we thought you could go to the pool with us. I can show you how to swim. Would you like that?' Georgiana had put the idea to Ed and, in turn, he'd suggested it to the Howells. Going to the pool would be a huge step for both her and the little girl, but they hoped in seeing her Hannah would recognise it was possible to still have fun with only one leg.

After considering the proposal Hannah solemnly nodded her head and everyone else in the room breathed a collective sigh of relief.

'Why don't we sit on the edge of the pool? That's okay, isn't it, Hannah?' Georgiana was perched poolside, letting her leg dangle in the water.

Apart from the lifeguard, they were the only people in the pool area, which Ed knew she'd appreciate. After their talk about her insecurities it was a move in the right direction for her to bare herself to these strangers. Even if she was wearing a modest one-piece.

Ed and Mr and Mrs Howell sat down too and Hannah watched them with sceptical interest from her mother's arms.

'Do you want to sit next to me, Hannah?'

Georgiana patted the space between her and Ed. After apparently deciding it wasn't a trick, Hannah clambered off her mother and scooted over beside Georgiana. Ed noted she was careful not to go anywhere near the water as she settled in between them.

Georgiana splashed her foot in the pool and Ed did the same.

'Do you ever have water fights, Hannah?' She playfully scooped some water over him, careful not to hit Hannah and upset her.

'Oh, she loves having water-pistol fights with her daddy. Don't you, Han?' Now her mother seemed to get the gist that they were trying to make her comfortable around water and started splashing her feet too.

This time Hannah nodded enthusiastically and shuffled closer to the edge. It wasn't some sort of phobia she had, at least.

Ed flicked some water back and showered Georgiana.

'Hey!' she shouted with good humour and retaliated.

Ed shook the drops out of his hair and scooped the water with his hand to soak everyone this time. To his delight Hannah was giggling at the exploits of the adults. It wasn't long before the poolside was a riot of squeals and splashes with little Hannah in the middle of it all. She was kicking her good leg in the pool, roaring with laughter every time she managed to splash someone.

They didn't push her too far out of her comfort zone, but he and Georgiana did compete in another race. This time without incident and with a cheering squad. It was their way of showing Hannah there was nothing to fear when Georgiana was just as able to swim as he was, even with only one good leg.

Step one was complete. Ed was willing to do whatever it took to get Hannah's hydrotherapy started. Recovery here wasn't a series of tick boxes. It took as long as necessary. With Georgiana's input he was sure Hannah would be back on her feet when she was ready.

'If you don't mind, I'd like to stay on in the pool for a while,' Georgiana said as the Howells got ready to leave.

'Not at all. We've got an appointment with the physiotherapist next. Perhaps we'll see you later.' Hannah's father stopped her from feeling too bad about not seeing them off because she wanted to enjoy some more pool time.

'Call by my office before you go.' It seemed

Ed wasn't going to get out either as he waved the family off from the pool.

'You don't have to stay on my account. I promise not to drown or break anything if you have work to get back to.' It was bad enough she monopolised his time at night without doing it during office hours too. She simply wanted some swim time to chill out after her earlier nerves about meeting Hannah and her family.

'It's not always about you, Princess. I have to exercise or I don't get to eat my junk food. For the record, our private session will be coming to an end and I don't know how much longer we'll have the place to ourselves. There will be other patients booked in to use the pool for the rest of the afternoon. You know, if you're not comfortable with anyone else seeing you here.' With that he pushed away to do a non-stop lap of the pool.

'It's fine. I've got over that hurdle now.' What difference was it going to make now if she was joined by other people who were likely more concerned with their own recovery?

She'd barely got the words out of her mouth when they were joined by one of the therapists and her patient. Their privacy was over as the rest of the clinic were granted use of the facility too. Georgiana carried on with her swim as the man was lowered into the pool on the hoist, knowing he'd be every bit as self-conscious as she was, thinking someone might be watching. She did, however, nod an acknowledgement to his anxious family member looking on.

When she'd been having her hydrotherapy sessions she'd done them alone. There were some who had family and friends to support them, but there were plenty of others like her who'd chosen to go through their recovery on their own. Looking back, she could see how much harder that had made things for her mentally. That had been the beginning of her pushing everyone away, rejecting any support. Her time here at Ed's clinic had shown her the benefits of having someone in your corner, shouting their encouragement and providing a sounding board for those struggling with their mobility.

The woman was walking up and down the length of the pool urging on who Georgiana assumed was her husband. Ed had been the one doing that for her lately. Perhaps if she'd had someone like him from the moment she'd been injured she might have found it easier to deal with the events. As much as she hated what her body had gone through, if it hadn't been for that bomb she would never have met Ed and she was grateful every day that he'd come into her life.

The patient was oblivious to the cheer squad as he continued his swim but Georgiana was fascinated. That outpouring of emotion, with no hint of self-consciousness, from the partner in pursuit of her husband's progress was something her family had never displayed even in the most traumatic of circumstances. Until recently she hadn't thought much of it, but now that level of support seemed the most important thing in the world.

Her envious surveillance proved invaluable when she saw the woman falter, a look of sudden distress crossing her face. Georgiana swam in her direction to make sure she was okay, just in time to see her drop to the ground and begin fitting on the floor.

'Ed!' She yelled for help, hoping he could get to her quickly.

His head jerked up to see what had made her call out. Then all hell seemed to break loose.

'She's epileptic.' The husband shouted from the pool, clearly frantic that he couldn't get to her side without help. Ed was swimming so hard towards the side of the pool he didn't seem to be taking a breath between strokes.

The woman's body was jerking and twitching uncontrollably, then she just seemed to roll into the water.

Horrific screams echoed around the walls and Georgiana wasn't sure if they were coming from her or the husband as they watched her fall helplessly into the watery depths of the pool. The lifeguard dived in and between him and Ed they managed to haul her leaden body to the surface. They kept her head tilted back to keep her face out of the water so she wasn't inhaling any more water. There was no way of knowing how much had already gone into her lungs or what damage she'd done when her head hit the floor. Georgiana knew from painful experience how hard those tiles were against one's skull. She'd been lucky not to have suffered anything more than an egg-shaped lump but a serious head injury here could have caused a skull fracture or damage to the brain.

Georgiana climbed out and shuffled over on her backside to help pull the woman out as the men pushed her from the pool. Those exercises to strengthen her muscles came into effect as she hooked the woman under her arms and pulled with all her might. She lay her down on the floor and tilted her head back to check her airway as the men scrambled up beside her.

'She's stopped fitting but I don't think she's breathing.' Georgiana couldn't feel a pulse and even with her ear to the woman's mouth she couldn't hear anything.

'She's bleeding too.' Ed pointed out the increasing pool of scarlet spreading out across the once pristine white tiles.

'Starting CPR,' Georgiana called. The most important thing was to get her breathing again. She started chest compressions, putting her hands on top of one another, interlocking her fingers and pushing the heel of her hand hard into the woman's chest.

'I'll get the defibrillator.' Ed took off, barefoot and wet, to track down the essential equipment.

This was the sort of life-saving emergency Georgiana was trained for so she was able to remain calm while the husband was crying and his therapist was shouting about having called for an ambulance.

The lifeguard, who she'd made redundant, made himself useful by covering the patient with towels to keep her warm.

Apparently Georgiana hadn't lost this instinct, this mission to save lives. It was something she didn't want to ever lose when it could prevent a family from the heartache of losing a loved one. She thought of the team who'd saved her. Though she'd lost a limb, she would be grateful for ever that they'd worked hard enough to make sure she had another chance at life.

Ed came rushing back with the portable defibrillator they obviously kept here in case of such events. 'We need to get her dried off and away from the water.'

Between them they made sure it was safe before they deployed the machine.

She heard it whir into life as Ed unbuttoned the woman's blouse and prepared to do his bit to save her too. He ripped the backing off the sticky pads and attached them to the woman's skin on each side of her chest. 'Stop CPR.'

'Stopping CPR.' Georgiana leaned back on her heels and let the machine take over, analysing the patient's heart rhythm. She and Ed waited until the shock had been delivered and instructions were given to continue CPR before they touched her again. They took turns between the shocks being delivered until the woman began to show signs of life. She tilted her head to one side and coughed some of the water out of her lungs.

The adrenaline coursing through Georgiana's veins during the high-pressure event was allowed to subside now she'd successfully done her part of the work. Ed's smile said he felt the same. It was down to the paramedics and the hospital staff now to take over but every joint medical emergency and patient interaction was bringing her and Ed closer together. As well as making her believe she was more than a victim. She still had a purpose, a skill that was needed, even if it was in a very different environment from the one she'd been used to. Her life was changing again but hopefully this time for the better.

'Maybe for your next appointment you should bring some water pistols.'

'Thanks. I'm sure she'd love that.' Hannah's father scooped her up in his arms as he thanked Georgiana for giving her a reason to return to the pool. They'd stopped by Ed's office as promised to say their goodbyes. Thankfully they'd missed the poolside drama and it was only Ed and Georgiana who were coming down off the adrenaline high.

'Maybe I should've asked Mr Lawrence about that first.' Georgiana laughed.

'That's fine by me. Always happy to take part in a water fight.'

It gave Ed a warm glow because this was going to aid Hannah's progress and was also an indication Georgiana intended on sticking around. He was getting used to having her here.

'Thanks for everything, Miss Ashley.' Mrs Howell went to shake her hand then emotion apparently took over and she threw her arms around her. Georgiana's expression was priceless.

'Any time,' she gasped, through the embrace.

'And we swear not to breathe a word to anyone.' Mrs Howell pretended to zip her mouth shut, making it clear she'd keep her word. This was their secret, their private club to which no one else was invited. Georgiana Ashley was another part of their daughter's recovery process and they wouldn't do anything to jeopardise that.

'You too, Doc. Thanks for setting this up.'

'No problem at all.'

Another round of thanks and goodbyes and suddenly Georgiana and he were alone in the room.

'That went better than I expected,' he said, waving them off before closing the door.

'Yes. I thought she responded really well. Maybe you should buddy up some of the adult amputees with the new patients so they can see what they're working towards.'

'If you're volunteering for future appointments, I'll take it.' It was a long shot but having her around would be a boost for everyone who came through the clinic doors.

He included himself in that bracket when they were already spending so much time together enjoying each other's company. To Ed she fell into neither of the two categories he seemed to divide his time into—work and family. She was a refreshing change from responsibility and being with her gave him some sense of having a life of his own outside those areas.

She glared at him with that 'don't push your luck' vibe and for once Ed knew when to shut up.

'What happens as the children grow? Do they get adjustable legs or do they have to be refitted?' Georgiana was holding up the different samples he'd brought in to show Hannah. Some of which were so tiny it was difficult not to be affected.

She was a compassionate woman so it was natural she should be thinking of Hannah and those like her.

'It's hard for the kids. They're being constantly refitted. There are the sporty ones who really need specially adapted limbs, but it's an expensive business with limited funding from the government. Unfortunately, I don't hold any sway in that department. I can mention it in the right ear but I'm not certain my input will help in any meaningful way.'

'You've been a great help with the charity, and look at how much you've done for Hannah's family.'

She gave him the side eye. 'That was a chat. I didn't achieve anything other than an interest in my leg. I can do that with anyone if I walk down the street in a pair of shorts.'

'You underestimate the influence you have. We have all tried in vain to get Hannah to co-operate and within a few minutes of meeting you she's suddenly engaged and excited about the prospect of a new leg.'

'Not everyone is going to respond to me in the same way as a four-year-old princess-mad little girl.'

'You're a member of the royal family, a soldier and a medic. There's plenty of reason to be impressed by you. You could be a great asset to the team here.'

'What do you mean?'

'You were great with Hannah. She related to you. Saw herself and what she could achieve. None of us have been able to get her near the water or to get fitted for her prosthetic. You could make that big difference to people's lives you wanted by being here. Would you like a job?'

CHAPTER SEVEN

GEORGIANA ALMOST LAUGHED in Ed's face at
the suggestion of becoming his employee but
the least she could do was hear him out after
everything he'd done for her. Before he'd
come along she would never have believed
she could sit and discuss her prosthesis with
strangers as though it was the most natural
thing in the world. She supposed it was now.
Although talking to one family was very different from revealing all to the nation. The
subject of many a nightmare.

'You want me to work here?'

'It's a possibility.'

Georgiana didn't know if the following
pause was for dramatic effect or if he was
expecting her to shoot down the idea immediately. She wanted to hear more before she
did that. When he realised she was listening
he carried on.

'You could be a mentor or train as one of

our aqua therapists.' Ed was fidgeting with the paperwork, rolling it up into a tube, then unfurling it again, until the ends were curled up like the fallen autumn leaves lying outside.

'This isn't some made-up position you think I need to give my life meaning, is it?' She didn't want to get into the details beyond the title until she could be sure it was more than a vanity project for her.

'No. Absolutely not.' Ed's stern denial and matching frown left her under no illusion that he was deadly serious.

'Good. I prefer people to be upfront with me. I've had enough of duplicitous people.' Life would be so much easier if people were more transparent with their agendas. It could have saved her brother for a start.

'I don't have time to play games with you, Georgiana. You should know by now I'm not someone who will pander to you to make you feel better. Nor would I lie to you.' He reminded her of their first meeting when he was anything but convivial. Ed had been pushy, confrontational but never patronising or sycophantic. She'd met plenty during her royal duties who possessed those particular qualities and Ed certainly hadn't made that list.

'What would it involve? I'd need you to lay

it all out for me.' She wanted to believe Ed that she could make a difference in the lives of people who were in the same position as her, but she needed more convincing.

'It could be a long night and that's something best discussed on a full stomach. I'll order some takeaway then I'll take you through everything.'

'Sounds good to me.' So good her heart gave an extra kick at the promise of having dinner with him after office hours.

When the food arrived a short time later, Ed shoved all the paperwork to one side. The only thing greater than his work ethic was his appetite.

'All this comfort food can't be good for you. Not that I'm complaining. It's a long time since I indulged in some fast food.' Georgiana was already salivating with the smell of fried chicken. It wasn't the same when the palace chef attempted to replicate it.

'I usually eat at home with my folks, so these past nights have made a nice change for me too. At least I don't have to listen to stories about the garden exploits of next door's cat or get a list of jobs to do around their house.' He ripped the paper bags open to use as a makeshift plate on top of his desk and proceeded to unpack the goodies.

'I'm the lesser of two evils? Honestly, I'm not sure my conversation is any more stimulating.' She was messing with him but deep down she was touched he was doing this for her. Taking time out from his family to spend it with her. Yes, they were discussing his work tonight but last night had been all about her. Each time he made sure they had sustenance to get through. None of which was in his job description.

'Trust me, it is. It feels as though I actually have a social life when I'm with you.'

'Ah, yes, you said you weren't involved with anyone.' Georgiana was intrigued by the idea of Ed's past loves, probably more than she should be.

For all the time they were spending together she knew virtually nothing about him. It wasn't fair when he knew all her dark secrets, or at least most of them.

'I was with someone for a while—Caroline—but I guess I wasn't putting the time into our relationship that it needed to work.'

Time. That was a word he used a lot, as though he didn't have enough of it. Yet he was always available when she needed him. It raised all sorts of questions about his home life and she hadn't forgotten he'd spoken of personal commitments. She was sure it wasn't a child he was talking about because he would've told her and he wouldn't have been so accommodating if he'd had a little one to get home to.

Perhaps he had a house full of cats to take care of, to feed and to empty litter trays. The image of Ed as a friend to felines amused her, but she hadn't seen one single cat hair stuck to his clothes.

One of the most frustrating things about him was that he was even more guarded than she was about his personal life. If she was to have any thoughts about going into business with him, she needed to know more about the man inside the business suit.

Ed was a good man, hard-working and incredibly easy on the eye. It was hard not to be attracted to him. Even more so the longer she spent in his company.

'Now, where are we eating? Here or on the floor?'

In keeping with the informal nature of the evening she went with the second option. She was loving the fact that he didn't see their time together as a chore or part of his charity work. Especially when he was fast becoming the highlight of her day.

Being with Ed was a taste of normality and she didn't have to pretend about anything when she was with him. Sometimes she wished they'd met under different circumstances. Pre-amputation.

He sprawled out on the floor next to her, his long legs parallel to hers with the parcel of food sat between them.

'You're a homebody, then?' She steered onto the topic of his family to detract from her wandering thoughts as she helped herself to a breadcrumb-coated drumstick.

'More through circumstance than choice,' he said, grabbing a handful of fries. Georgiana had to wait until he'd washed them down with a gulp of cola before he explained. 'I'm the eldest of six. Mum and Dad worked full time and when my youngest brother was born with spina bifida they had their hands full taking care of him. It fell to me to look out for the others because they spent so much time at the hospital for his surgeries and treatment. I guess they got used to me in the carer role. My siblings are married with families of their own but I stayed to take care of our parents. They're getting on in years now. Then there's my little bro, Jamie, who, despite his insistence he doesn't need me hanging around, I like to keep an eye on too.'

It was more about his personal life that he'd shared in the interval before his next bite of food than in the entire time she'd known him. She could see how the implications of his circumstances filtered into every other aspect of his life once she read between the lines.

'Is that what caused the friction between you and your ex?' She could imagine that fighting for his attention against his responsibilities to his family and work could have been demoralising. Yet, he'd been able to find time to fit her in. Perhaps he hadn't been with 'the one'.

Why did that give her a glimmer of heartless satisfaction and where did she rate in his priorities alongside a girlfriend? These were questions that were going to plague her later and she knew why. She liked him. More than she should for someone she'd only known for a few days and she wanted to believe it wasn't one-way traffic. Nothing could come of it, she understood that, but it would be nice if he found her desirable in some way.

'In hindsight, she put up with a lot. Quality time as a couple ended up at the bottom of my priorities. With work and taking care of my family, I was never there when she needed me. Perhaps I should've tried harder, or maybe I'm just not cut out for relationships if I can't give someone what they need from me.'

'Relationships are tricky at the best of times but when you've got complicated family matters going on too it's impossible to make them work. It's not as easy to walk away from family as it is a relationship. I should know. I joined the army to distance myself from mine, yet here I am, back living with my parents. Any chance of suitors is a distant memory.' She consoled herself with another bite of fried chicken. It had been an age since she'd been with anyone and longer still since any meaningful dalliance. She'd had too much going on with her home life and her army career to consider anything serious.

'It's not as though you've moved back into a terraced house where you're all living on top of each other. You live in a palace. Don't expect me to feel sorry for you.'

She mirrored his good-natured grin. Ed wasn't afraid to call her out on things like that. He didn't pander to her and made sure she stayed grounded, not caring she was royalty. However, that insolent comment deserved a suitable reaction.

She lobbed a chip at him, which he managed to catch in his mouth.

'Show-off.'

'Are you going to tell me what caused the rift between you and your parents? It's none of my business but they do seem to genuinely care about you.'

Georgiana couldn't argue with that, despite their differences in the past. They'd gone out of their way to adapt the home for her coming back. Even if she had seen it at the time as resignation that she was changed for ever. At least she'd had somewhere to retreat to when coming to terms with everything. Their actions were only beginning to sink in now her emotions weren't so fraught.

What Ed was asking her to do was spill the family secrets. Something her parents had gone to great lengths to cover up. However, telling him what had happened was more about honouring Freddie than betraying anyone. Her appetite abandoned her as she thought about it all.

'I expect you heard about Freddie's death a few years ago.'

'Your brother? I remember reading about it. I'm sorry. He was very young to have died so suddenly. It was his heart, wasn't it?' There was the gut punch. The story that had been fed to the nation and the one she was about to blow wide open.

'In a roundabout way...' It was heart failure listed as the cause on his death certificate but it failed to detail the circumstances of her dear brother's last tragic hours.

She knew she had Ed's attention when he stopped gnawing on the chicken bones.

'You don't have to tell me if it's too painful.'

'No, I want to. Someone should know the truth.' It was on the tip of her tongue to ask him for his discretion but given his loyalty to her thus far it would've been an insult. Especially when he'd laid his own personal life bare only moments before.

'If this is something I need to sign a non-disclosure agreement for before I hear it, you might want to rethink that idea.' He offered her an out, most likely aware of the significance of the event itself as well as what it was taking for her to confide in him. This story would earn a fortune in the wrong hands. Thankfully, she was aware of how safe and strong Ed's hands were.

'I trust you.' The words almost caught in her throat, her body trying to hold onto them because she was so unused to saying them.

He wiped his hands on a napkin and sat up straighter. 'I'm listening.'

Georgiana closed her eyes so she could see a picture in her mind of her brother in happier times. It was getting harder to remember Freddie before he succumbed to the darkness hounding him but there he was, smiling back at her. They were physically alike—he was tall and willowy with a shock of dark hair— but that was where the similarities ended.

His wardrobe choices were more flamboyant than hers. He had a wicked sense of humour where Georgiana had been the sensible one of the pair. Trying to keep him out of trouble and usually failing. He had as much trouble accepting their limitations as part of the royal family as she did. Only he'd kept his pain mostly to himself. If she'd known, if she'd been able to help him stand up to her parents and the regime that rejected the idea of a prince who didn't fit in with their ideals, he might be here now calling her Hopalong or something equally inappropriate.

When Georgiana opened her eyes Ed was watching her intently. He held out a hand to hold hers.

'Are you okay?'

She squeaked out an affirmative. With the unexpected physical contact and his eyes full of concern, she didn't think she could hold it together for much longer. So, she got straight to the point.

'Freddie was gay.'

Ed was still holding her hand.

'He never came out to us but we all knew. We all pretended otherwise. A gay prince didn't fit in with tradition, you know?'

'I can see that.' His hand on hers gave her the strength to carry on no matter how tough it was in the retelling.

'He did his best to conform for our sake but he must've been so unhappy.' Her voice cracked as she imagined the pain Freddie had gone through, knowing he wasn't wanted in his truest form.

Ed scooted forward so his knees were bent and he was face to face with her. 'I'm sure that wasn't your fault.'

'I didn't do anything to help. He clearly didn't think he could talk to me about anything or ask for my help. It was an overdose. None of us saw it coming. Afterwards, none of us were allowed to discuss it. Instead of raising public awareness about the issues of mental health or some introspection about what had led him to take his own life, we were supposed to sweep it under the carpet. A tragic accident if anyone asked. They didn't learn anything from Freddie's death and kept on pretending everything was fine. I couldn't take any more.'

'That's when you joined the army?'

'Yes. I wasn't prepared to play along any more. I needed to separate myself from the whole suffocating regime. None of us are perfect but we have a right to be happy. A right to be ourselves. I signed up because I wanted to do something meaningful and make a difference.' She wasn't sure she'd achieved anything except prove she couldn't escape her destiny as part of the royal family.

'I'm sure you did to the men and women you served alongside. You certainly did with Hannah and her family today and I'm sure you will with the rest of our patients. You're an amazing woman, Georgiana.' He was so close to her, saying all the things she needed and wanted to hear, and it was all she could do not to bury her head in his chest and lose herself in his embrace. She'd been strong for so long on her own and Ed was the one person with whom she could let go. He'd take care of her if she asked him to. Goodness knew she was close to doing so.

The office door suddenly burst open and Ed dropped her hand as if it were suddenly something contagious. A tall, owlish man a good ten years younger than him stood staring at them.

'Sorry. I didn't realise you were here. I saw the light on.'

Ed jumped to his feet and helped her into a standing position. 'We were running through a few ideas for the clinic. Georgiana, this is my partner, Giles.'

There was that moment all too familiar to her as he pondered how to react to the introduction. To save any awkward attempt at a bow she stuck out her hand first.

'Pleased to meet you.'

A look of relief flashed across his face as they shook hands. 'It's an honour to have you here. I heard you made quite an impression today. Welcome on board.' Giles was beaming at her. It made her irrationally happy when Ed had made out he was a difficult man to please.

'Thanks.'

'If I'd known you were still around, Giles, I'd have saved you some chicken.' Ed gathered the empty takeaway cartons and dumped them in the waste bin.

Giles wrinkled his nose. 'No, thanks. I'm sure we could've arranged a proper meal for our visitor, Ed, if you'd told me we were entertaining.'

Georgiana did her best not to smirk at the glare Giles directed at Ed, promising to have this out with him later.

'It's fine. It's not often I get to eat "normal" food.'

'Yeah, she's slumming it with the common people tonight. Eating with her fingers on the floor instead of silver service in the banquet hall.' It was difficult to tell which of them Ed was teasing, her or Giles, but this time she wasn't the one rolling her eyes at him.

'In that case I'll leave you to it. Lovely to meet you, Ms Ashley.' This time Giles did give a half-bow before he took his leave.

'I don't think I've ever seen Giles quite so awestruck. I think I should keep you around for a while.' Now she knew it was her he was teasing she didn't mind when he was talking about continuing their association. It wasn't a doctor/patient set-up, nor was it strictly speaking a working relationship. The truth was she didn't know how to describe their pairing and that made it something new and exciting.

'Why, thank you. I'm truly privileged.' She also enjoyed the jovial atmosphere they cultivated so easily. Ed didn't alter his personality to suit her. Something rare in her social standing.

'He'll be calculating how much our shares will go up if we have a princess on staff.'

'Well, he seems very charming. He definitely has better manners than you.' Georgiana crumpled up a rogue fries packet left on the floor and tossed it at him but his quick reflexes saw him catch it easily.

'Ouch, and after I pulled out all the stops to impress you.' He clutched his chest as though fatally wounded. This man was too much. Too funny, too pretty and way too much of a complication for her heart to be all of a flutter.

'We've had dinner and annoyed your partner. Is it time to call it a night?' Regardless of the crush she was having on Ed here, she didn't want to outstay her welcome.

The realisation that was what was happening made her glad he couldn't see her blushes. It wasn't that he'd given her any indication that he saw her as anything other than another project. Apart from the way he'd come to her aid in the pool, bought her dinner, twice, and held her hand earlier. *Oh.*

'I hope not.' Before she could overanalyse his every look and touch as much as her own, Ed came to stand beside her. She was so aware of him now the air between them seemed thick and charged with something new.

'I meant what I said earlier. I'd love you to be a mentor here. If you'd prefer something on a full-time basis I'd be happy to take you on at the clinic if you wanted to retrain in a medical capacity?' His belief in her was intoxicating. He really thought she was capable of anything. Such a contrast to those who'd written her off. Including herself.

'I'll think about it. Tell me more about the charity you're setting up. Other than talking to people and getting funding for prosthetics, what else do you have to achieve?' There needed to be something long term to sustain the momentum.

'I had toyed with the idea of a sports event. There are games held for disabled athletes and wounded veterans but I thought we could have something similar for our kids. Eventually branching out into an international event.'

'That's a brilliant idea.' She thought of all the other people who'd had their dreams stolen from them with the loss of their limbs and who needed something else to focus on rather than the life left behind.

By first bringing Hannah to her attention, Ed had given her a renewed sense of purpose and achievement. To the point where she wanted to continue that work. They could do the same for others by introducing this sports programme.

'It would take a lot of organisation and dedication.'

'I'm sure you're up to the challenge.'

'I hope so. I thought we could get some of our well-known athletes with disabilities to help with motivation or even training.' He produced a list of recognisable names.

Now she'd got to know Ed it was clear he thought much more about others than himself. As if he needed any more brownie points in her eyes. At this rate she'd be starting a fan club for him before too long.

'I might be able to get some veterans on board. I met quite a few at the rehabilitation unit.' It occurred to her that, so far, she wasn't contributing a whole lot to this meeting except for making eyes at her colleague.

'That would be fantastic. The more inspirational mentors we have who've experienced the same struggles as our patients, the more they'll benefit.'

'I'll get in touch with some of my old army buddies and see what I can come up with.'

'If you can get a list of people together who are willing to participate I can show it to Giles.'

'I get the impression he doesn't know that this is happening?' Ed had been careful not to mention any of this in his presence.

'He's aware I have an interest in building a charitable arm for the clinic so I would have to consult him. However, I'd prefer to present it to him as a fully formed plan.' He was already scribbling notes, his mind working overtime on how to make it all work. Georgiana admired his dedication. Among other things.

'If you don't mind me asking, why are you doing this? I mean, obviously it's going to help those families who couldn't otherwise afford to fund these things, but what's in it for you?' It wasn't that she thought he was doing it for accolades or recognition for his altruism, but she was interested to know what drove his passion for it. For her it was a deeply personal issue on many levels.

She could relate to those going through the process of amputation and rehabilitation. Ed was already so in demand to those closest to him—she didn't dare include herself in that group—it didn't make sense why he'd take on another time-sucking task.

'I told you about my brother, Jamie? Well, we were told he'd never be able to walk. I think in the old days they wrote you off if you had any sort of disability. Our mother and father put as much time and effort in with him as they could to stimulate him, did physiotherapy with him. If they'd sat back and accepted his limitations he wouldn't be living a normal life now.'

'It was their dedication that pushed him to break those boundaries they were told to expect.' Georgiana suspected it was also down to their loving eldest son, who allowed that to happen. He'd said he'd practically raised his other siblings. Although he didn't see it as a sacrifice of his childhood since it had allowed his brother to have one too.

'Exactly, and I want these children to have every opportunity to do the same. Make every therapy, each new bit of technology that could enrich their quality of life, available to them. Money shouldn't be an obstacle to a child fulfilling their potential. I'm not in this for me or the clinic. This is for every child who has had a difficult start in life like my brother. Every loving family who wants the best for their babies.' His impassioned speech, coming from so deep within his heart, left nowhere for him to hide his feelings. Eyes filled with liquid emotion and voice wobbly, he was drawing from his own heart-wrenching experience watching his brother's fight.

In that moment she could feel his passion, his pain at being so powerless at the time and a vulnerability in him she would never have expected to find. Ed was a man who loved unconditionally.

'It sounds as though you went through a lot.'

'It was Jamie who went through the operations, the bladder problems and the skin irritation. Everything that comes from living with spina bifida. It was my parents who put the extra time into his physical activity. Taking him to all his appointments so he could reach *his* full potential. Not everyone has such supportive parents.'

'Or such an amazing big brother.'

Ed ignored the praise. 'There are kids with the condition who'll never walk, but some have more use of their legs. We saw some families who either didn't want to, or simply couldn't, give the same time and commitment to their children with extra needs. They're the ones who need the most help in later life. Jamie can get about most days without assistance and lives independently. Everyone should have that chance. The same goes for the children who want to get involved in sports and it's only the matter of money stopping them from fulfilling their potential too.'

'That's all very admirable but you don't have to do it all alone, you know.' Georgiana could see and hear what was driving him to work so hard on the behalf of others, but she worried he was doing it at the expense of his own needs. He'd already lost one relationship over it.

'Says Miss Independent,' he countered with a sardonic smile to make her laugh.

'Yeah, I know, but I've had this really irritating voice in my ear for days now making sure I stop feeling sorry for myself and get out of the house.'

'I'm an irritating voice? Wow.'

'You know I'm joking. Without you I'd still be locked in my room doing my Greta Garbo impression.'

Her 'I want to be alone' motto was becoming more like 'I want to be with Ed' these days.

Ed shrugged. 'I could see your pain but I also understood that need to do everything yourself. It seems easier to do things that way. Then you're the only one who gets hurt.'

She related so much to everything he was saying. They'd both chosen to shut themselves off from the world rather than run the risk of getting hurt again. 'Yeah, but look what we've achieved together. Ethan, Hannah's family and that woman at the pool—we worked as a team to save the day. It doesn't always have to be a bad thing to get help or ask for it. You've taught me that.' The smile on her lips was interrupted by the touch of Ed's as he leaned forward and kissed her.

Eyes closed, heart hammering, she shut out everything around her except the soft pressure of his mouth on hers. It was unexpected but it also seemed natural after they'd been so intimate with their emotions. She sighed into the kiss, enjoying the sensation and excitement of exploring this new development with him.

All of a sudden that delicious pressure was released. She opened her eyes to see Ed had moved back, looking stunned, as if he'd been zapped with a thousand volts of electricity.

A creeping sense of unease made its way through her body. Rather than wanting to make mad passionate love to her, he was pulling away from her.

'Ed?' All her insecurities came rushing back. Why on earth had she thought a handsome, kind doctor would be attracted to a woman with so many obvious issues? He'd probably only kissed her because he felt sorry for her. She hadn't been subtle in her admiration of him.

Georgiana got up, wanting to escape any

further humiliation, but Ed was there before her, blocking her exit.

Before she could dodge around him and bolt for the door, Ed was cradling her face in his hands, smiling at her. 'Stop talking.'

This time she did as she was told and let him kiss her as if he meant it. As if he'd been holding back the first time and now he was letting the bubbling well of desire come to a boil. His arms were locked around her now, holding her tight to him as his mouth found hers again and again. Hard and insistent. Soft and tender. Sending her mind and body into a whirl.

She melted against him, let him fold her into his strong frame like the delicate princess she was supposed to be. Except princesses weren't supposed to be trying to rip a man's clothes off, desperate for him to remind her what it was to be desirable.

Ed groaned as Georgiana untucked his shirt from his trousers and slid her hand under the fabric. Searching hands found their way confidently across his abdomen. He sucked in a shallow breath at the intimate touch. It had been some time since he'd last engaged in this kind of fevered display. It felt good. He hadn't been sure that she was attracted to him in any way, yet her playful tongue in his mouth, her apparent determination to strip him of his clothes would suggest differently.

Deep down Ed wondered if she was searching for affirmation she was still attractive when she was so hung up about her altered appearance. In satisfying her craving for male interest, he might've been anyone. For him, though, this moment would only have happened because of the strong, courageous person he knew her to be. From the moment he'd seen her pounding the treadmill, defying those who'd tried to steal her independence, her life and her femininity, he'd been lost. There was nothing he wanted more than to clear the contents of his desk onto the floor and take her right here, right now, but that would cause more damage than satisfaction.

An ill-advised tryst would endanger everything they were working towards. Getting in deeper with Georgiana could only end in tears for a multitude of reasons. For a start she was a princess and he, for the want of a better word, was a commoner. It would cause the sort of scandal she wanted to avoid. She was also vulnerable, not in the right head space for romantic involvement. He'd be taking advantage to continue this. With all their plans, they were going to be spending a lot of time together and there was no room for tension between them. Which was bound to happen when he had so many other commitments. History had told him so. He'd been here before, only this time they were both loners. Making a future together as a couple was impossible.

Yet it was hard to put a stop to something he was enjoying so much. Hard being the operative word.

'Georgiana…we…need…to…stop…before… this…goes…any further,' he said in between passionate kisses. He slipped a hand around her waist, pulled her in for one last, long, lingering lip lock before letting go and stepping back, breathless and wanting.

'Whoa.' He had to hold onto the edge of the desk until he got his bearings again, the adrenaline rush of having her in his arms and subsequently letting go knocking him off kilter.

'What? What's wrong?' Her dilated pupils and kiss-swollen lips only increased his level of guilt because he still wanted to kiss her.

He should've shut this thing down instead of selfishly prolonging it for his satisfaction. It took all his resolve not to oblige her sweet mouth begging for more.

'Nothing's wrong, it's all so very right,'

he said regretfully, 'but that's not why we're here.'

'Right,' she said, blinking furiously, trying to focus.

'Neither of us is in a position to start something. You're going through a lot of life changes and, as I've told you, my home situation is already demanding. It isn't a good idea.' He didn't want anything to compromise the work they'd been trying to do together. Georgiana was helping him so much with the gala, then there was the possibility of her working at the clinic. His libido couldn't be his motivating factor when an inevitable break-up would impact on all areas of his working life. There was no way he'd jeopardise the futures of his patients just so he could have some fun.

'It's no big deal. Just a kiss. It doesn't have to mean anything and it certainly shouldn't impact on our plans here. Let's never speak of it again.' She was trying to make light of it but her eyes held that sadness that came from rejection.

It was difficult to ignore what had happened when he was buttoning his shirt and tucking it back into his trousers, his skin scorched where Georgiana had sought him.

'It'll probably take a few days before I can

report back on those veteran guests we talked about. I'll get back to you with details when I can.' She was letting him know she'd be out of bounds for a while, which wasn't a bad thing considering what they'd been up to. At least with some space they might be able to forget it, put it down to a lapse in judgement and leave it in the past.

If only he could forget how she tasted on his lips, felt in his arms and set him on fire everywhere she'd touched him.

'Let's get you home.'

Out of my office, out of my head and out of temptation's way.

CHAPTER EIGHT

'I'D LIKE TO talk to you about something.' Missing the company she'd had at the clinic, Georgiana had taken to sitting with her parents in the evening. Ed had put their nocturnal activities on hold under the guise that he needed to finalise arrangements for the gala dinner. It was probably for the best when there could be no future for them together and she didn't want to spoil the relationship they already had.

Since the incident in his office they'd been careful not to be alone together. As agreed, they hadn't referred to it again. It didn't mean his lips weren't still imprinted on hers or that her brain would let her forget how incredibly hot it had been when he'd kissed her.

'Of course.' Her mother set aside the book she'd been reading and gave Georgiana her full attention. She was out of her sick bed now, a little delicate but well enough to get around indoors at least.

Georgiana cleared her throat, anxiety having taken up residence there and threatening to block her airways. In talking to Ed about his family, telling him to reach out for help, she'd have to do the same. To move on she was going to have to confront the past. With her parents. Asking them to acknowledge their mistakes in order to help her.

'I've been sneaking off to Mr Lawrence's clinic to use the gym equipment there.' She thought honesty was the best way to begin.

'Oh.' Her mother formed a perfect 'O' with her lips.

'I hope that's all you've been doing.' Her father was frowning at her from his armchair, his newspaper now abandoned on his lap.

This conversation had been easier in her head when she'd been rehearsing it.

Georgiana swallowed hard as illicit images flashed guiltily into her mind of the other thing she'd got up to with Ed at the clinic. 'Not all, no.'

'We don't need any scandal.' He scowled at her, his reaction making her all the more eager to have this conversation.

'Everything's entirely above board. I've been helping him out with a patient, that's all, but it has made me think about everything that's happened since my surgery.' She was building up to say things she'd been holding inside for years. The air in the lounge was thick with anticipation, as though the very walls of the palace were waiting for her to speak her truth. Her parents were silent, listening for whatever she had to say. The clock on the mantelpiece behind her ticked away the seconds and the fire crackled and spat in the hearth, urging her to get a move on.

'We're very proud of you, my dear. Everything you've achieved since coming home is, quite frankly, remarkable.' It was unexpected praise from her father, not known for outbursts of sentimentality, but it wasn't what this was about.

'That's the first time you've said that to me.'

'I'm sure it's not, Georgiana. We are astounded by the progress you've made.' Her mother chimed in but the praise was offset by the cast-upon look on her face. As though she were the one who'd been wronged.

'But you've never said it. That's my point. We haven't actually sat down and had a conversation about how this affects us.'

'I think we're managing fine. You're back

on your feet and, with Mr Lawrence's help, I'm sure you'll fully recover.'

'No, Mother, I'm never going to fully recover. My leg isn't going to grow back, is it?'

'Don't be facetious, dear.' Her mother sniffed.

'I'm serious. It's gone and I'll have to wear a prosthetic leg for the rest of my life. There's no point in pretending otherwise. We have to accept that or at least acknowledge it.'

'There's no need for that, Georgiana. We know perfectly well—'

'Then for goodness' sake talk about it.' She cut off her father's scolding, years of pent-up emotions breaching all notion of civility. 'I had to hear it from Ed that you were concerned about me enough to ask him to intervene. Why not come to me and ask me what I need from you instead of going behind my back?' Georgiana hadn't realised how much it had hurt to hear that until just now. All that time she'd been here believing she was all alone in her recovery, her parents had kept up that façade of cold indifference to cover their concern. At a time when she'd needed comforting, needed them, more than ever.

Her mother was fidgeting with her hands in her lap, unwilling to meet Georgiana's eye. 'You didn't seem to want us anywhere near you and you're so strong we knew you'd pull through.'

'That didn't mean I didn't need you to tell me you loved me, that you'd be proud of me no matter what happened.'

'It goes without saying, Georgiana.' Her father wasn't any better at understanding her point than her mother.

'No, it doesn't. Did you ever say that to Freddie? No. None of us did. He took it as confirmation we were ashamed of him and his sexuality. To the point he believed we wouldn't miss him if he took his own life.'

'It's not our way to be demonstrative with our feelings. You know what's expected of us, and you, in our position. Blaming us for whatever was going on in poor Freddie's troubled mind isn't going to bring him back.' Her mother was dabbing at her eyes now. Lord forbid she'd be seen shedding a tear over the son she'd lost. Georgiana was beginning to think she was fighting a losing battle instead of making reparations with her parents.

'What's more important to you? Keeping up appearances or your family? You've already lost a son because you wouldn't face up to reality. Freddie was gay and he killed himself because he knew you could never accept it. There, I've said it.' She was breathless as the words poured out of her on a tide of emotion. These were things that should have been dealt with long ago but she was as guilty of hiding from the truth as they were, when she'd joined the army and left the country rather than face this.

'I know, I know.' Her mother was openly weeping now and Georgiana's father went to comfort her.

'The loss of your brother was unbearable, Georgiana, and we didn't see the point in dragging his name through the mud by releasing the details. It didn't mean we were ashamed of him. We wished we'd done more for him, been more, but regret won't change history. Your mother has been worried sick over you too, aware that you're pushing us away. Tell us what we can do so we don't lose you too.' The plea from her father was more than she'd expected when she'd opened this dialogue, but she hoped it was the beginning of the healing process for all of them.

'This. Being honest with me. This is the first time you've acknowledged what happened to Freddie.' A huge weight lifted from her so she no longer felt that chest-crushing pain every time she thought of her brother and the betrayal they'd unknowingly taken part in.

'I think about it every day. I don't want to lose you, Georgiana. This will have to work two ways. You need to tell us how you feel. How we can help. It's going to be a learning curve for us.' The words coming from her mother's lips were everything she'd wanted to hear for so long and her father was nodding his head in agreement with every word. It was going to take time to build the sort of relationship most people had with their families but time she had. They owed it to Freddie to make this work.

'For me too. I'm making a lot of changes. I'm going to take advantage of the second chance I've been given at life. Freddie never got one.'

'We let you both down. Instead of trying to mould you into the people we thought you needed to be, we should have let you be the amazing people you are. I'm sorry we realised that too late for Freddie.' Her mother was sobbing now.

'I'm sure he knew you loved him in your own way.' They'd all made mistakes, none of which could be rectified now. All they could do was hold their hands up and move on. Something her parents were apparently willing to do.

'Our thinking and parenting came with the

vision of what we should be as role models. Not what our children needed from us.'

Georgiana understood what her father was saying and realised they'd tried to be supportive even if they hadn't always known how to demonstrate that.

'I appreciate everything you've tried to do for my recovery here. It's really what set me on this path, helping out with the gala and thinking about my future again.' Along with the introduction her mother had engineered between her and Ed. Not that Georgiana was going to give her credit for opening up her heart again when there was every chance it would get battered the next time she met him.

'It's an amazing thing you're doing, helping those children.'

'Thank you, Father. It's not all my doing. Ed… I mean, Mr Lawrence is the one who put it all into motion.'

Despite promises to herself, her feelings for him hadn't diminished since she'd taken some time out from him. She'd justified the break in face-to-face conversation by telling herself she'd confused friendship and compassion for something more. Except she couldn't get him out of her head.

When it came to helping people, he was always first in the queue. A man who could be relied upon to do the right thing. That was exactly why he'd put an end to the fabulous kissing, regardless of how hot and bothered they'd been. They had to put the charity and the clinic before their own wanton needs. Unfortunately.

Now the gala dinner was only a matter of days away she would have to see him again, along with the rest of the world. The publicity was a necessary evil to get the charity off the ground, but she was willing to sacrifice her vanity for the future of their patients.

'You and the doctor seem to be close these days,' her mother said nonchalantly, not fooling Georgiana for a second that she wasn't interested in anything that might be going on.

'You know he's been opening the clinic for me at night and we've had stuff to sort out for the charity.' Georgiana brushed off any insinuation there was something more than professional interest there, but she was finding it impossible to maintain eye contact with the lie.

'He's a good man, I'm told. Very honourable.' That had to have come from her mother for her father to talk about someone he'd never met in such glowing terms.

'Yes, I'm sure it wouldn't have been his idea to sneak you out of here like a thief in the middle of the night.' Her mother's accusation was directed at her.

'Actually, it was a joint enterprise.' Ed had been the first to suggest sneaking her out, but she'd followed up on the idea. They'd both been complicit. It made her laugh to think of the absurd picture their exploits would have made to a spectator. At the time her freedom was everything and Ed had gone along with it all. Who knew what it would've cost him if anything had gone wrong? Yet he'd done everything she'd asked of him. Whatever it took to make her comfortable in a world she thought she no longer knew. He'd been her rock and she was missing him dearly when she'd been so enjoying their time together.

'My rebellious daughter.' Her father chuckled.

The build-up to the gala was exciting but also terrifying. It was going to be her big reveal to the country and she wanted Ed by her side for that. She could get through it on her own—she was strong enough to do anything after all she'd survived. The difference was she wanted him there with her. Everything was better when he was around.

'Is Edward escorting you to the gala, dear?' Again, her mother's astuteness astounded her. She wondered if this was a recent thing now her parents had decided to try harder to be involved in her life or something they'd both chosen to ignore until now.

'He'll be there. We haven't discussed the logistics of it yet.' Since it was being held in her family home, she wouldn't have to make a dramatic entrance. Therefore, she was under no pressure to have a plus one as she arrived at the event. Something she knew would've been under scrutiny and a strain on whatever fragile relationship they had left, if at all.

'Don't you think you should? It's only a matter of days away. You can't simply leave these things to chance. Have you even spoken to a stylist about dressing you for the occasion? You want to make a good impression.'

Georgiana read that as, 'You'll want something to detract from the ugly fake leg.'

'I've chosen my own outfit. I promise I won't embarrass you. This is too important to me.'

'We know. Be true to yourself, that's all we want for you.' Her father retrieved his tumbler of whisky from the mantelpiece and raised it in her honour.

Georgiana frowned. 'Okay, who are you and what have you done with my real parents?'

Instead of taking offence, her mother actually laughed. 'I know it's hard for you to believe, Georgiana, but you're not the only one who's had a life-changing experience. Losing your brother and not knowing if you were going to pull through really made us appreciate the time we have together. We'll do whatever it takes to make you believe that.'

'I believe you,' she said, her voice barely audible. If she'd given them a chance to prove themselves when she'd first returned, they could have had this conversation then. Instead of appreciating the changes they'd made, adapting the house, she'd shut herself off from them. Ignored the changing world around her to focus on the negatives she'd have to live with.

In the same way her injuries had made her reassess her life, they'd also caused her parents to rethink what was important. She was thankful she apparently topped that list. Not many had the support she'd taken for granted until now.

The emotionally charged family love-in was in danger of becoming awkward. She feared there was a group hug coming, or, worse, a mass sobbing. The attempt her parents were making to understand her state of mind and implement changes to their attitude showed they were doing their best to relate to her. Trying to break out of the old regime, which didn't fit with the modern world. That was all she could ask of them.

Ed was tearing his hair out trying to manage everything at once. With the gala only two days away he was attempting to organise his time better between work and family. He wasn't succeeding. His dad had been on the phone about the hospital appointment he'd promised to drive him to. He had patients queuing up for consultations, which was a good thing businesswise, but he was time poor at present.

It didn't mean he wouldn't give anything to be with Georgiana again. By kissing her he'd been playing with fire and he was the one left burning. He should've stopped it but he'd fed the fire. Now he was suffering the after effects. He was missing her and had even resorted to texting her an inane message asking what colour she'd be wearing on the night so he could co-ordinate with her. Just so he could have some sort of communication with her. Not that she'd replied.

He'd left himself the lion's share of the organising to do, with Georgiana doing her bit at a distance from him. Goodness knew he was out of his depth organising an event at the palace to kick-start a brand-new charity. Talk about pressure. Pressure he'd put himself under by not sharing the load with anyone. She was right, he had to learn to reach out to people where he could and stop doing everything by himself. It wasn't a weakness to ask for help and certainly didn't make him any less of a good son or brother if his every waking moment wasn't devoted to them. Jamie was a grown man now, living his own life. Perhaps it was about time he did too.

He thought about Georgiana and what she was prepared to put herself through to help him and the charity and was humbled by her courage once more.

It was one of the many, many qualities he admired in her. If nerves were getting the better of him, he could only imagine how she was feeling. Yet he knew she'd come through for everyone concerned. He hoped, in being open about what had happened to her, she'd benefit as much as those they were raising funding and awareness for.

He heard some commotion out in Reception and attempted to ignore the increasing level of noise, hoping Giles or Security would take care of it. There was too much for him to do without getting into a row out there. When the sound of feet thundered down the corridor, he knew he'd have to go and investigate.

'What on earth is going on out here?' he demanded as he made his way through the growing crowd of staff and patients. Even though he'd been preoccupied he was sure he'd have heard a fire alarm going off. Although the gasps and excited whispers whooshing around the crowd led him to believe that nothing life-threatening had happened.

'Excuse me. Pardon me.' He eased his way through to the eye of the storm, where he was confronted by a mass of mobile phones vying for a photo op. Bewildered, he looked to Giles, who was grinning like a loon beside him. 'Have I missed something?'

'I think Christmas has come early for us.' He gestured towards the door, where everyone's attention was focused.

In that second Ed was as spellbound as all those around him. A smiling Georgiana was holding court, resplendent in a chic white trouser suit and surrounded by men in black with earpieces and walkie talkies.

She hadn't spotted him yet, busy chatting with a young man in a wheelchair who was clearly as infatuated with Georgiana as Ed. She always looked beautiful to him, but she was glowing as children lined up to say hello to her. He didn't know what had prompted an official royal visit but he was smiling from ear to ear because of it.

She was agreeing enthusiastically with whatever the teenage girl next to her was saying and gave her a hug before straightening up again. That was when Ed caught her eye. His breath caught somewhere between his lungs and his throat when she beamed back at him.

'Sorry about all the disruption, Mr Lawrence. I was coming to pay you a visit but the parents decreed I bring the circus to town with me this time.' She shrugged apologetically.

'No problem. We can go to my office if you want. I think there's room for your bodyguards.' After their last encounter he wouldn't be surprised if she'd brought them along for protection from him.

'I'm sure we can manage a conversation without them.' Her knowing wink said she knew exactly what he was referring to but she wasn't holding anything against him. More was the pity.

'You know where to find me when you're ready.' He began to make his way back to his office, expecting her to take her time with her appreciative audience. Those clamouring to meet her were sure to give her a confidence boost after her time out of the limelight. It was also a good trial run to stabilise her nerves before her big night.

'Thanks, everyone. It's lovely to meet you all. I hope to see you again soon,' he heard her say before following him down the corridor.

Her minders were herding the crowd back, giving her some room for a conversation in private. It was only on seeing her in action that Ed remembered who it was he was dealing with. Georgiana Ashley was a princess and he'd had the audacity to kiss her like a man possessed.

He kept a few steps ahead, so he was able to make some attempt at tidying his desk before she came in.

'Take a seat,' he said, pointing to the chair on the other side of the desk, maintaining an acceptable distance between them.

She closed the door and sat down. 'This wasn't supposed to be a whole "thing". This is why I resorted to sneaking out. It's much less hassle.'

'But this is safer. I do think you've made everyone's day here. Including Giles. You know news of this visit is going to spread like wildfire?' So far she'd been so opposed to the idea of people even knowing she was back in the country they'd been playing hide and seek with palace security. This move was on the very opposite end of that scale.

'I'm aware of that. Why do you think I didn't turn up in my workout gear?' She rapped her knuckles on the prothesis hidden beneath her trousers.

'I suppose it will garner interest leading up to the fundraising campaign.' People were going to want to know why she'd come to this specific clinic and, as much as he didn't want her to get hurt, they needed the publicity. Every penny counted in helping these families.

'I thought that too.'

'Oh.' He was at a loss for words that she'd gone to all this trouble in person when they'd been conducting all of their conversations over the phone since the last time they'd been alone in here.

'I thought I'd pop in and say hello before the big night. I wasn't sure what you'd be wearing, though, when you said we'd be colour co-ordinated. I'm wearing blue, so does that mean you'll be in a blue bow tie and cummerbund or were you going to go the whole hog in a matching sky-blue tuxedo?'

Teasing him with that mischievous look on her face wasn't doing anything to prevent him wanting to kiss her again.

'I was thinking head-to-toe blue. Maybe with a side split in the trousers.' One kiss and he was completely gaga over her. He was pretty sure he wasn't managing to hide it either.

'Should I come pick you up? Hire a limousine? Buy a corsage?' He hadn't been on the dating scene for a while and he didn't know the etiquette for courting a princess. Not that they were dating, but he would be escorting her.

She was laughing at him again. He obviously wasn't cut out for the escort business either. 'It's not the prom, Ed, and I live at the palace, remember? I'll see you there.'

'Right. I'll get there early to help with the catering or whatever else needs doing.'

'There's no need. My parents have everything in hand. They've been very supportive with regard to the event.'

Ed didn't know if he'd ever not be preoccupied again when in the same room as Georgiana, that kiss never to be forgotten.

'It sounds as though you're making real roads to getting your relationship back on track. Excellent news. I'm so pleased for you.'

If she had her parents to turn to again the onus would no longer be on him to provide support and that was what he wanted, wasn't it? That he wasn't spending so much time thinking about her. Then why did he have a sudden sinking feeling in the pit of his stomach, thinking this gala night could be the end of something beautiful?

'Speaking of which, I should get back and help organise the flower arrangements, seating and all of those important details my mother will be freaking out about.' She rose to go and, as good manners decreed, Ed stood to open the door for her. Before she left she placed a hand lightly on his chest and kissed him on the cheek. A barely there, ghost of kisses past, which still managed to make a significant impact. She hesitated to move away and Ed held his breath. If she decided to kiss him again he was no stronger to resist than he had been the last time.

When she did step back and finally walk away all the oxygen in the room and in his lungs went with her.

He was in big, big trouble.

CHAPTER NINE

'I THOUGHT YOU might like to wear this.' Georgiana's mother placed the intricate silver tiara on her head. With delicate entwined vines and leaves, encrusted with tiny diamonds and sapphires, it wasn't as ostentatious as some of the crown jewels but none the less beautiful.

'Thank you. I look like a real princess now.' She thought about little girls like Hannah who would be expecting her to look the part and she had to admit this was one perk of the job.

'It was your grandmother's from when she was young and beautiful like you.' Her mother kissed her forehead and Georgiana felt the love radiating from her in waves. Being at home these days was so much more pleasurable now they were all doing their utmost to communicate and pull together as a family. Although tonight she was flying solo.

'I'm nervous.' This was her first official

royal engagement but she also had the added pressure of introducing the charity for Ed. She didn't want to mess anything up for him.

'I still get stage fright about these things but such is the life of royalty. Anyway, I have great faith in you. You'll dazzle everyone in the room.' Her mother kissed Georgiana on both cheeks once she'd finished her pep talk as her daughter prepared to go into battle with her insecurities.

Georgiana was grateful for the support and would never dream of taking it for granted again when it had played such a huge part in her recovery so far. When she'd first woken after the amputation, she'd never have believed she could walk out onto a stage in a room full of people to tell her story. She hadn't done it all on her own either.

'I really want to make you and Ed proud.'

Her mother pulled her into a hug. 'You're the best thing in our lives. We love you very much and you make us proud every single day just by being you.'

She released Georgiana from her grasp again. 'As for Edward, surely he's as smitten with you as you are with him. How couldn't he be when you're so amazing?'

'Mother!' she spluttered. 'I've told you, we work together, that's all.' Her conscience burned with the lie and the memory of their clinch.

'Uh-huh.' Her mother's arched eyebrow said she wasn't convinced by her protestation otherwise.

Deep down Georgiana knew what she was saying was true when she'd fallen hard for Ed.

'I should probably go down.'

As per her mother's advice she'd waited until all the guests had arrived before she made her entrance. Along with being protocol for the royal family to be the last to arrive, it meant all the gawping and gossiping would be over in one go.

After another hug and a deep breath, she descended the staircase and waited as her presence was announced to the assembled guests in the grand ballroom. She'd improved enough over the weeks that she was steady on her feet but she longed to be on Ed's arm for that extra security.

'Her Royal Highness, Princess Georgiana.'

She caught the end of the announcement, heard the clatter of chairs as people got to their feet as she made her way to the front of the room.

The number of curious faces staring back at her was overwhelming. She waved and smiled but she was close to walking back out. Then she saw Ed on the stage, handsome in his black tux and clapping her approach. She focused on him and glided past the round tables occupied by patients, veterans and possible donors. He met her on the steps and offered his arm, which she clung to gratefully.

'You look amazing,' he whispered into her ear, giving her that final boost before facing her demons.

'Did you change your mind about the blue suit?'

'I decided it wasn't my colour. It looks so much better on you.' He was full of much-needed compliments.

She took her place at the podium, her hesitation magnified at the microphone before she finally found her voice. 'I may look a little different from the last time I saw you. I've had some cosmetic surgery since then.'

To illustrate her point she stuck out her leg and the cloud of billowy fabric slid away to reveal her prosthetic to the crowd. She'd chosen the sky-blue, off-shoulder number deliberately. It was embroidered down one side with silver flowers and sequins, which spilled down onto layers of chiffon. The intentional, sexy side split was on the right-hand side, effectively revealing her prosthetic leg to the world and facing the last of her worries. There was no going back now.

The combination of awkward laughs at her joke and gasps was better than dead air. This wasn't about feeling sorry for herself and she didn't want people to do it for her either. The event and the charity were about improving the lives of the children like her. It was supposed to be an uplifting speech so she remained positive about the things they could do for children who'd lost limbs due to accident or illness. She kept it short with only a small reference as to how she'd lost her leg to prevent any speculating.

Between her and Ed, they'd agreed she would give a brief introduction to the charity and her involvement, before the dinner. He was in charge of the later presentation complete with moving footage of patient stories and their plans for a national sports competition. So as she came to the end of her spiel she'd be able to enjoy the rest of the evening along with everyone else.

'If there's one thing Mr Lawrence and his clinic have shown me it's that missing a limb doesn't have to mean missing out on life. With your financial support, Love on a Limb can make this a reality for dozens of children who otherwise might not have the

of insecurities and, at times, innuendo and he considered himself damn lucky.

From what he'd seen everyone had had fun. Fantastic raffle prizes had been donated and won, dinner eaten and conversation had flowed. With the business aspect of raising money out of the way, it was time for him and Georgiana to enjoy what was left of the night.

They'd brought in a band to end the evening on a high. As they began to play their soft, smooth melody, Ed reached out a hand to Georgiana, who was about to take her seat after another round of schmoozing.

'Would you care to dance?'

'Pardon? Are you sure you're asking the right person?'

'The only person I want to dance with here. I'm sure you know how to do it better than I can.'

'I haven't done it since my operation. I'm not sure I can.' There was panic in her eyes but she took his hand all the same. That display of trust in him touched Ed's heart. He didn't want to do anything with the potential to embarrass or hurt her, but he thought she should enjoy every second of the night. It was as much hers as the charity's.

'I hear it's like riding a bike.' It was the sort of comment guaranteed a sardonic response but it was designed so she'd be too busy slamming his joke to worry about anything else.

He was right—they were on the dance floor before she was mid eye-roll.

'Is everyone watching?' she asked as he took her in his arms.

'I hope so. I didn't put on this tux to be ignored.'

She slapped his shoulder but she was laughing, the last of her anxiety slipping away.

Once they'd led the way, others followed until the floor was full and they were lost in one another's arms without a care.

'It's been a good night.' She was resting her head on his shoulder, the sweet scent of her perfume invading his senses and filling his lungs.

'I'm glad you've enjoyed it and that I was here to share it with you.'

'You know, it doesn't have to end here…'

He looked down at her to make sure she was saying what he thought he was hearing. 'Are you sure?'

There was no point in denying he wanted nothing more than to spend the night with her any more. They'd gone past that and with the gala out of the way they might be able to spend more quality time together. He didn't know where things would lead to, only that he wanted to give it a try.

'I've handed back the crown jewels, I've chatted with my old army buddies and stopped hiding the truth of who I am from them and everyone else here. I think I'm ready for bed now.' The nibbling at her bottom lip gave away something of her nerves but she nodded her head regardless. He grabbed her by the hand and led her off the floor.

'In that case, let's get these people their coats.'

The one thing he could hear above the roar of blood in his ears was Georgiana's giggle. It only made his heart beat twice as fast and his patience last half as long.

He didn't know what was happening to him, but for the first time in his life he was making himself and his needs a priority. It might seem selfish but Georgiana was the only good thing to come into his life in a long time and he didn't want to lose her when a few days without her felt like an eternity.

This could be his one chance at happiness and nothing was going to get in his way when she'd made it explicitly clear she wanted him too.

* * *

'What do we have to do to get these people to leave?' Ed was a warm breeze in Georgiana's ear but he still made her shiver.

'Shh. They've paid out a lot of money tonight. We can't very well tell them to clear off because we have better things to do.'

'Like each other,' he growled and made her melt at the animalistic tone of his desire.

As time went on, her bravado was beginning to ebb away, letting anxiety flow back in. She wanted to sleep with Ed; it was the next step for them. It was the personal significance she was having trouble with. This would be the first time she'd been naked with anyone since her life, and her body, had changed for ever. Though she wouldn't want it to happen with anyone else, it was nerve-wracking having sex with someone for the first time and this was so much more than that. There were other things to consider besides her desire for him. Not least how she would adjust to her new lopsided body during the act.

'Princess Georgiana would like to offer her gratitude and say her goodbyes,' Ed announced to those still congregated in the foyer.

'Goodnight, everyone. Thank you all for

your support,' she managed to say before being whisked off back towards the ballroom.

The room was thankfully empty now. It had been a lot to go from isolation in her room to hosting such a large crowd in a few weeks. Although it hadn't been as scary on the night as she'd imagined. Most people simply wanted to know how her prosthesis worked and whether or not it was painful. Given the reasons they were all here tonight, she'd been only too happy to engage in those conversations.

Ed closed the door behind them and before she had a chance to speak he had her pinned against the closed door, kissing her the way she'd been imagining all night.

She groaned against his lips with the satisfaction of tasting him again, of having his body pressed tightly to hers. He moved his mouth across her cheek, kissed her neck, and sucked her earlobe into his mouth. *Oh.*

'Are you sure it's okay for me to stay? I don't want to cause you any problems,' he said, kissing the spot behind her ear that sent tiny electric shocks to every one of her erogenous zones.

'I'll just say you had too much to drink and couldn't drive home. There are dozens of bedrooms you could've stayed in if anyone asks.' They hadn't done much to hide their blossoming romance and she was sure tongues would be wagging about the princess and her handsome surgeon, but she didn't care. She'd spent too much time worrying about what people thought and Ed had shown her how much more fun she could be having if she concentrated on what it was she wanted. Tonight, it was him. In her bed. With her.

'As long as you're sure.'

'I love that you're being a gentleman but you should know by now I'm a woman who knows her own mind.' She reached up and tugged on his bow tie, loosening it along with her inhibitions.

He grabbed her wandering hands with his before she started undoing his shirt buttons.

'I get that, but I think we'd be more comfortable in the bedroom. I don't want to rush this in case someone finds us. I want to take my time with you.'

It had crossed her mind that it might be less awkward as her first time since the amputation to do it here, clothed, standing and quickly but his promise to take things slowly was too much to resist.

'Do you think they've all gone yet?' She was breathless with desire; all social etiquette faded into insignificance when he was kissing her all over.

'I bloody hope so.'

The ache inside her was so great she could only agree with his statement.

They checked the coast was clear and, with only catering staff zipping about collecting their stuff and the band loading their instruments into the van parked outside, they'd got their wish.

'Bedtime?' Ed slipped his arms around her waist and claimed her, setting off fireworks in her belly.

'Bedtime,' she confirmed, entwining her fingers around his so he knew this was a joint decision. He brought her hand to his mouth and kissed it. This was going to be all right. Ed made everything feel good.

Georgiana didn't remember climbing the huge staircase hand in hand with the man in front of her. The promise of what was to come propelled her in a daze, so she practically glided to her bedroom with him. The place where she'd been seeking solace for the past few months was now going to be the site for another historic event. One she hoped was going to be more positive and fun to look back on.

He tilted her chin up and placed a kiss on

her mouth. A long, tender, swoon-worthy display of his intentions for the night. She was already a puddle of arousal before they'd even got naked.

With her help his jacket hit the floor. She whipped the loose bow tie from around his neck and tugged his shirt free of his trousers. All the time not taking her mouth from his. She needed that contact to stop her from worrying about what was coming next. As long as he was kissing her, wanting her, everything would be all right.

She heard the rasp of her zip and felt the air on her bare skin. Her breathing, which had been shallow and rapid, now seemed to have stopped altogether. This was the moment she'd thought she'd never be confident enough to experience. She'd thought she'd never be attractive to another man again. Ed's body, pressed so tightly against her, was disputing that for her.

Her hands were frozen, still clutching his shirt as he eased her dress away. She watched his eyes follow it to the floor. Not once flinching or showing anything but appreciation and lust. She could breathe again.

'You're beautiful.'

Once she let the compliment sink in she

saw no reason not to repay the favour, un-buttoning his shirt and tossing it on the floor.

'In a hurry, are we?'

'Only to get you naked.' Her bravado was returning full force as she exposed him piece by piece.

'Be my guest,' he said, letting her strip him completely.

It was important for her to have some con-trol of this moment and divesting him of his clothes was the best way to do that for now.

She'd seen him at the pool, yet the taut muscle and smooth contours of his body were still a revelation. While she was busy ogling him, Ed undid her strapless bra and buried his head between her bare breasts. If he wasn't careful, he was going to render both her legs useless when she was becoming a liquid mess beneath his touch.

'Ed, you're killing me here.' It was all she could do to remain upright, giving her no chance to explore his body as much as she wanted.

His response was to knead her breasts and suck hard on her nipples until her knees fi-nally buckled. He caught her and carried her over to the bed. His every gesture, their every interaction since they'd met had been building to this and she was ready to burst with the heady anticipation of the night ahead.

He slowly inched her silky knickers down her legs until she was completely naked and open to him. There was only one thing spoiling everything for her. At this time her prosthetic seemed ugly and unnecessary but she didn't know how to remove it without spoiling the mood. Ed slid a hand there, attempting to remove it for her, but that was a humiliation too far. She tried to stop him but he silenced her with another kiss.

'Let me. I've done this a hundred times. Not in this scenario but you know what I mean.' They broke any potential awkwardness with their laughter. Ed's touch was so deft and gentle she hardly noticed what he was doing until he did the unthinkable. He kissed his way along her injured leg as though it was simply another part of her to be explored and appreciated. Those ridges and bumps where the surgeons had sewn her back together were now a map for his lips to follow. So gentle, so loving in a place more intimate than any other part of her body. Somewhere no one else had ever touched her so tenderly. Ed turned the most damaged part of her into something beautiful. A part of her she no longer needed to be ashamed about.

Tears burned behind her eyes but only for a second as he kissed his way towards her inner thigh and made her forget what was making her so emotional. Her head and her body now just a mass of sensations to enjoy.

The quick darting motion of his tongue along her sensitive skin made her quiver, her limbs trembling more the closer he came to her most sensitive spot. When he found her wet and waiting, he met her with his tongue, sending shudders of exquisite satisfaction wracking through her whole body. She was completely at his mercy, waiting for his next touch. He delved deeper, pushing the limits of her restraint, seeking only her pleasure.

The bedsheets were bunched in her hands as she clung to the last of her sanity. Then he hit that perfect spot that made it impossible to hold back the flood any longer.

She cried out until her throat was raw as Ed created wave after wave of pure pleasure at the tip of his tongue. He didn't stop his pursuit until he'd wrung every last drop of her climax from her.

When she came back down to earth she was dazed and unable to move a muscle. 'My body's like lead.' She giggled as the man between her legs raised his head.

'Is that a good thing?' He gave her that

cheeky grin of his, full of pride at his accomplishment.

'You know it is.' She was sapped of all her strength, weak from the sheer force of her climax, and she couldn't have been happier about it.

'You're looking particularly smug, Princess.'

'So are you, Doctor.'

'And we haven't even had the main event yet.' He crept further up her body, completely covering her with his, bracing himself either side of her.

At the promise of more, certain parts of her came back to life, reawakened by the tender, loving kiss he left on her lips. She wrapped herself around him and he buried himself inside her with a satisfied grunt.

Her gasp as he filled her was only the beginning. Each stroke as their bodies collided again and again, all the accompanying kisses he gave her, were met with a satisfied moan.

Ed was so attentive to needs she wasn't aware she had, spoiling her, giving her everything she wanted and more. She'd never felt more like a princess in her life.

They hadn't discussed the future beyond tonight but she didn't see how they could carry on as though nothing had happened after this, when he'd changed her whole world.

Until tonight Ed had told her he hadn't wanted to mix business with pleasure. Family came first, work a close second and relationships didn't even make the list. Yet Georgiana knew when she was with him, she wasn't a misfit with no place in the world. She was a mentor, a medic, an ambassador, and along with all that he made her feel like the most desirable woman in the world.

As she and Ed reached that peak of absolute bliss together, their cries of ecstasy echoing each other, she knew she'd lost another piece of herself. Her heart.

CHAPTER TEN

GEORGIANA'S FIRST INSTINCT when she woke up was to reach for Ed. She had a smile on her face, remembering their conscientious exploring of the limits and logistics of an amputee's sex life. Until she was confident it didn't make the slightest bit of difference about her leg when making love with him. She was awestruck to discover that she still had a fully functioning sex drive and he made her feel as though she was the most important person in the world every time he'd kissed her during the night. Her body was thoroughly ravished and pleasantly numb this morning.

'Morning, sleepyhead,' she said, trying to rouse the naked figure sprawled across her bed. As pleasant as the sight was, they couldn't lie here all day.

'Hmm...?' A drowsy Ed rolled closer to her, his eyes still closed. It was no wonder he was exhausted after she'd put him through his paces last night.

'We should get up.' Her sigh was filled with longing and regret that their night together had to come to an end.

'Why? We still have some time before we have to go to work,' he mumbled into the pillow.

The way he said it so casually made her smile. As if they were any other couple about to start their day together. It had taken some time and soul-searching but she had a role now. One that was about more than just making personal appearances and news headlines. She had a purpose again. The talk with her parents and, later, the gala had given her so much hope about her place in the world. Okay, it wasn't the one she'd had, or had expected to have, but she wanted to capitalise on her sense of achievement.

Ed had given her the platform and confidence to address her issues in public but it was down to her to continue the momentum. There was so much more she could achieve using her position. She saw no reason why she shouldn't become an advocate for other charities and use her voice to get recognition where it was needed. As a representative of injured veterans and the amputee community she could do a lot to raise the profiles and funds for those who needed it. After months of floundering, not knowing where she'd be wanted and accepted, Georgiana believed she'd found a new path that would incorporate the princess and the soldier in her. She was keen to embark on this new life outside these walls. The one she'd been avoiding for so long.

'With everything that happened last night, I'm going to have to release a press statement.'

Ed snapped awake, his big blue eyes sparkling with mischief. 'There's really no need. I know I was good but you don't need to tell the whole world about it.'

Georgiana rolled her eyes. 'You've every right to be full of yourself this morning. Last night was…amazing. But I was talking about the gala. Word will be out about my injuries and I'll have to work with the palace to give an official statement about what happened and what it means to my position as Princess and next in line to the throne.'

'Surely you have a little time to fool around first?' He slipped his hand under the covers and swept it over the curve of her hips.

She groaned, tempted to surrender to her libido in place of her common sense. 'I really wish I did, but I have an appointment with my aftercare team first thing too.' Something her visits to the clinic had prompted her to do. She'd seen the importance of having regular check-ups and maintaining contact with the team who'd taken care of her. Her appointment today was to check out some recent discomfort she'd been experiencing. Probably the result of the extra workouts and busier lifestyle putting more strain on her body. No doubt they would tell her to take it easy.

Ed immediately sat up and cupped her face in his hands, his eyes searching her face for the truth. 'Is everything okay?'

The concern she saw and heard from him sent her heart fluttering and she leaned into his touch.

'I'm fine. It's just a check-up.'

'Do you want me to come with you? I could move a few things around—'

'Honestly, there's nothing to worry about, but I don't want to miss the appointment. We really should get moving.'

'You want me to go?' He pulled her in for another one of those deliciously long and passionate kisses she was trying—and failing—to deny herself.

'No, but if you don't I'll never leave this bed.'

'Is that such a bad thing?' He was kissing his way down her throat now and nibbling away at her defences.

She gave it considerable thought and came to the conclusion that she'd quite happily spend a lifetime in bed with Ed.

But could he spend a lifetime with her?

Georgiana wished she could live in his arms for ever and the pang of longing lasted after he'd dressed and left her bedroom looking dishevelled and gorgeous.

The news from the hospital sent her into something of a tailspin.

'Complications…bone spurs…further surgery.'

One appointment reminded her that nothing was permanent and an amputation didn't mean her health problems were over. Resuming her royal duties, training for a new job and a future with Ed could be in jeopardy and she didn't think she'd recover from losing everything again.

It wouldn't be as serious an operation as before. The abnormal bone that had grown around the end of her amputated limb was causing pressure points where it met her prosthetic. If refitting didn't help, she was going to have to have surgery to remove the excess bone. The reality meant she was likely going to have ongoing problems and pain for the rest of her days.

She'd gone straight to the clinic to find Ed when her test results and X-rays had not been favourable. He was the one she wanted to go to. In keeping with their agreement, she'd let her parents know too but Ed was the one she needed to comfort her and tell her everything would be all right.

Although, this latest information might alter everything between them. They already had things to work out, when he seemed to have so little time to devote to a relationship. She didn't know what this latest development would mean to them as a couple. So determined was she to speak to him on the matter that even when she was told that Mr Lawrence was at his parents' place, Georgiana got her driver to track down the address.

'I think I'll be fine on my own,' she insisted to her team when they pulled up outside the unremarkable detached cottage far enough outside the city she was sure she wouldn't be spotted.

There was no sign of Ed's car outside the house but she made her way up the path regardless. If someone was at home, perhaps they could tell her where to find him.

It took so long for someone to come to the door after she rang the bell she'd convinced herself the house was empty. Then a dark shape behind the frosted glass moved slowly towards her.

Thankfully she recognised the senior Mr Lawrence who opened the door even if he'd aged considerably since she'd last seen him. His body was thinner, his complexion paler and his bent posture gave away the deterioration in his health in the intervening years.

'Mr Lawrence, I'm so sorry for intruding into your afternoon but I was looking for your son. Is Edward here?'

'Miss Georgiana. How lovely to see you. Come in, come in.' He shuffled back to make room for her so Georgiana didn't see a choice but to follow him inside.

He pointed her towards the door down the hallway, presumably because she'd get there faster than he would. She saw the stairlift as she passed inside and wondered why on earth they wouldn't move somewhere all on one level when he clearly had mobility issues.

'Marg. Miss Georgiana has come to visit,' he called ahead to warn of her appearance.

When Georgiana walked into the unbearably warm lounge she found Mrs Lawrence struggling out of her armchair. 'There's no need to get up. I just came to see if Edward was here.'

'Sit down and I'll go and put the kettle on. You just missed him. He was over earlier doing a few errands for us. We can't get about as much as we used to. Edward's a good boy. He's gone to pick up our prescriptions from the chemist.'

'Will he be back?' Georgiana followed her into the kitchen, where Mr Lawrence was pulling laundry out of the washing machine into a basket. The effort making him wheeze breathlessly.

'Let me do that for you,' she said, unable to stand by and watch without offering a helping hand.

'It's fine. I'll leave it there for our Edward. He'll peg it out for us when he comes back.' He straightened up as much as he could.

'Edward clearly takes very good care of you both.' She knew Ed wouldn't consider helping out a chore at all. It was apparent how much he loved his parents and he would do anything for them. But care for two elderly parents was a lot for one person to take on—could she really add to that?

'Oh, yes. He's always here for us. I wish we didn't have to rely on him so much, but age is getting the better of us these days. He's such a good son.' Mrs Lawrence fussed around getting her best china out and piling a selection of biscuits onto a plate.

Georgiana nodded as sadness wrapped her in its embrace. Ed had a full life. There for anyone who needed him but it didn't seem fair asking him to make room for her too. Especially when she was facing another surgery and an uncertain future. What if he was with her, caring for her, and something happened to his parents? Would he ever forgive her for diverting his focus? She wouldn't be able to live with herself knowing she'd caused him any unnecessary pain.

Mrs Lawrence let her husband carry the tea tray into the lounge. Georgiana followed with an even heavier heart than the one she'd arrived with.

She made small talk with his parents while they drank their tea and even forced down a biscuit to keep them happy. Though it was hard to swallow down along with the realisation of the situation. Ed was a man devoted to his parents and his patients. He had precious little time as it was and, when she faced potentially numerous health problems for the rest of her life, as much as it pained her, she couldn't expect him to dedicate any of that time to her.

'It was lovely to meet you both. Sorry I missed Edward but I really should be going.' She got to her feet, ready to escape the suburban life Ed enjoyed and she knew she could never have.

When Ed's father made an attempt to get up from his chair she held up a hand to stop him. 'Don't trouble yourself. I can let myself out. Thank you for your hospitality.'

They said their goodbyes and she promised to pass on their best wishes to her parents before she was able to finally make her way out. Only to find Ed pulling up outside the front of the house.

He got out of his car clutching a paper bag and wearing a smile on his face that unfortunately Georgiana couldn't replicate.

There was no way of knowing how long recovery would take after her surgery this time around. She might have to adjust all over again. Now she'd met Ed's parents, had confirmation he was stretched to breaking point already, it made sense for her to bow out of the picture. Especially when she was going to be incapacitated again for goodness knew how long. He already took care of everyone, his parents, his siblings, his patients; he didn't need someone else to look after. She couldn't add to that and she wouldn't ask him to. He'd already given her so much. She was stronger and more confident in herself because of him. But she couldn't keep relying on Ed to get her through. Some things she would have to do alone.

Ed was over the moon to see Georgiana. Leaving her bed this morning was one of the hardest things he'd ever had to do. Last night had been amazing, more than he could ever have dreamed of. Passionate, loving, experimental were all ways he could've described their first time and he certainly didn't want it to be their last.

Once she resumed her royal duties they were going to have to find some way of carving out some quality time together if this was going to work—and he wanted it to work.

Until meeting Georgiana he'd thought a relationship meant taking him away from his family, but he could see now he'd conditioned himself to be indispensable to everyone when they could survive perfectly well without him by their side twenty-four-seven. It could've been residual tendencies from his youth or a desire to spend the time with his parents that he'd missed out on when they were caring for Jamie, but he knew things had to change. It didn't mean he loved his family any less. Georgiana had gone to a different country to get away from her parents, but with some space and honest conversations their relationship seemed to be stronger than ever.

He realised he'd fallen for her and these days he lived for the moments they had together. It didn't mean he had to neglect anyone, he just had to make some changes to give them a chance as a couple. He'd begun with asking the pharmacist to deliver his parents' prescriptions from now on, taking advantage of a service he'd never considered before.

He was also planning to speak to his parents about hiring some home help. Choosing non-essential errands over the potential of a new relationship with Georgiana wasn't an option. Granted, good sex alone didn't equate to anything long term, but if he wasn't honest with himself about wanting a future with her he'd lose her.

He hadn't realised that until today. If he didn't take a long hard look at what he was doing with his life he could end up alone. He'd never been happier than when they were together. She represented parts of his life he'd neglected for too long—fun, companionship and love.

'Georgiana? What brings you here? Did you need me for something?'

'Nothing important.' She didn't seem as enthused to see him even though she must have come here to find him.

When he went to give her a hug she shrank back. It was such a change from last night when the only place she'd seemed at home was in his arms.

'Is something wrong?'

Her expression shuttered. 'We can't do this, Ed. You can't clone yourself to be in two or three different places at once. I knew the score from the start. Relationships come at the bottom of your priorities and now I... I'll put a strain on you even more. The clinic and the charity are too important to let personal issues interfere with your work.'

She sounded so cold, as if she'd already made her mind up that this was over, that Ed didn't know how to fight back. 'Why don't we go inside and talk?'

Georgiana shook her head. 'I've just taken tea with your parents and, if anything, it's made me see how much they need you. You'll be better off without me making demands on your time too.'

'My relationships in the past didn't last because it wasn't you I was with. I'm going to make changes, to make time for us. You know we could have something good. Last night was proof of that.' He went to reach for her again but Georgiana stepped back. For the first time in adulthood he had a real taste of how it felt to be alone.

'How much of a future do we really have, Ed? I'm next in line to the throne. When the time comes are you really going to give everything up to come and live my life? How can I even ask you to do that? How can I ask you to care for me if…?' Her hand swept down to her prosthesis as she trailed off. For the briefest of moments, he thought he saw pain in her eyes, but then her cool demeanour returned. 'We're dreaming if we think one night together means we're compatible.'

This time he did manage to catch hold of her arm and pull her to him. 'Do you want me to kiss you again and remind you that what we have together is amazing?'

His eyes were glittering with determination as she wrenched her arm from his grip. 'Don't make me call my security.'

'Oh, right. You're going full princess now, are you? Now you've got your confidence back I'm surplus to requirements?'

'Something like that,' she spat at him and shattered what was left of his heart and his dreams of a future together.

'So, this is it? You're ending this on the doorstep. No discussion?'

'We've had the discussion. You don't need me being a burden any more.'

'You mean you don't need me any more.' He'd watched her transform from that defensive, spiky injured vet to a confident princess in her rightful place. She'd always been strong, she just had to believe in herself. It felt as though he'd been hit by a truck, which then reversed over him to finish the job, discovering that she wasn't as invested in him and their possible relationship. All the time he'd spent convincing himself it was in his best interests to stay single seemed laughable now when Georgiana was the one who'd decided she'd do better on her own. With his past relationship history he didn't even bother to disagree.

'You're right. I don't.' She swept away from him, taking the whole new future he'd planned with her. Now he was the one who didn't know where he belonged any more.

* * *

It had been days since Georgiana had broken her own heart. She'd put on a stellar performance, pretending to Ed she didn't care enough to continue with their relationship, until she'd got home. Then she'd locked herself in her bedroom and cried until there was a possibility of her drowning in her own tears. She'd wept for another life taken away from her and for the pain and hard work she knew she'd have to go through again in recovery. Most of all she'd wept for the man she knew she'd loved. And lost.

In the spirit of their new, open relationship she'd confided in her mother about the operation she was due to undergo and what had happened with Ed.

'It's a shame things didn't work out. Mr Lawrence is a lovely man but it's important that you're happy, Georgiana. Although, at this moment in time you don't look particularly happy,' her mother had said when she'd literally cried on her shoulder over the breakup.

However, she'd picked herself up and thrown herself back into work even if she'd lost something of her pep in the aftermath of breaking up with Ed. No, she wasn't happy but she couldn't carry on simply doing as she pleased. What she wanted wasn't necessarily in Ed's best interests. Yeah, it would be nice to have him by her side for her operation and recovery but at what cost to him? She'd get over him. Eventually.

Today she was setting up a new LGBTQ charity her parents had suggested to honour Freddie. Another new milestone in their continuing evolution into the modern world.

She was surprised and not altogether pleased to find out she had a visitor to the palace. It soon transpired her mother hadn't been entirely transparent about her recent dealings and had set this meeting up before conveniently going off to make an appearance anywhere other than here.

'You're Ed's brother?' Now Jamie had introduced himself she could see the similarities in their build and colouring.

'Don't hold that against me.' He laughed at his own joke. That cheeky sense of humour apparently ran through the rest of the family too. He was a good-looking guy and clearly had the family charm, but he wasn't a patch on his older brother in her eyes.

'What can I do for you? You said you'd been speaking to my mother?' Georgiana's heart was racing with desperation to find out what had brought him here but decorum decreed she play it cool.

'Yes, sorry. I don't usually do this kind of thing. You know, casually turn up at palaces and expect an audience with the princess in residence, but the queen thought it would be a good idea. I mean, do I need to call you Your Highness or bow or anything?' He pointed at the crutches he was currently resting on, having declined her invitation to sit.

'I don't think we need to stand on ceremony if you have my mother's ear.'

'That's only because I begged and pleaded with my father to make the call. It was a family emergency.'

That pricked her ears up and, anxious for the news that had brought him here, she asked, 'Is Ed all right?'

'It depends what you mean by all right. He's still breathing and working as hard as ever but I think you've broken him.'

'What do you mean?'

'Usually all he talks about is his work and his patients. Then there was the charity and of course, yourself. Now we can barely get a grunt out of him. He even took time off to show our parents around some sheltered accommodation. This should be the happiest time of his life, getting some independence back, but he's as miserable as sin.'

'I'm not sure what you want me to do.'

'I love my big bro to bits. I don't know what we would have done without him growing up. He spent so many years taking care of us yet refuses to let us take care of him. Our Ed has a white knight complex. For him to make this change is a major deal. It's not a decision he would've made lightly and I'm sure he's done it for you.'

'I know he does a lot for your parents. I didn't ask him to stop.'

'No, but clearly having you in his life made him think differently about how he prioritised his time. I don't know what happened between you but I'm asking you not to give up on him.'

'It's complicated—' Her surgery was already scheduled. She wasn't going to tie him down by expecting him to take on the role of carer for her next.

Jamie rolled his eyes. 'I'd talk to him but he's stubborn. Short of staging some sort of intervention, pinning him to a chair and forcing him to open up about how he's feeling, I don't know how to fix him.'

'I'm not sure I'm in a position to do anything.' Georgiana didn't know where the surgery would leave her in terms of physical recovery and her future. Her circumstances since their last conversation hadn't changed, even if his had.

'My brother gives so much of himself to others, I think it's only fair you give him a chance to prove himself to you.'

Georgiana admired Jamie's devotion to his brother. She wasn't sure he'd approve if he knew, but it was touching nonetheless to see his love for his family was returned tenfold.

'I'm going to be incapacitated for a while but I think we do both need some closure.' By the time she'd had her surgery he'd realise what the road ahead held and any thoughts of beginning a carefree life with her would be well and truly put to rest.

CHAPTER ELEVEN

IN HINDSIGHT, Ed could have arranged driving lessons with an instructor for Jamie but he had nothing else to do with his time these days.

Until meeting Georgiana he'd thought a relationship meant taking him away from his family, but he could see now he'd been using them as an excuse not to get too close to anyone. It was too late now.

He groaned as he pulled into the car park and marched through Reception to his office, where he was picking Jamie up. Mad at himself and everyone else because he wasn't with the one person he wanted to be with.

'Are you ready to go? I haven't got all day. Some of us actually have work to do,' he barked at Jamie, who was spinning in his office chair.

'Who took a bite out of your biscuit? I

hope you're not this rude to your patients, big brother.'

'Not my patients, just family who take me for granted.'

'This was your idea, remember? I was going to take lessons and you said I'd save money if I let you teach me. Don't take out your bad mood on me.' He grabbed his jacket and his usual cheery expression had been replaced by a scowl.

'Sorry.' None of this was Jamie's fault. It was entirely his for not making space in his life for Georgiana sooner.

When they'd been together he'd had a life, an equal with a lot of things in common. He'd lost everything worthwhile now that she was gone.

'Why don't you go and talk to Georgiana, sort out whatever is keeping you two apart?' Jamie ruffled his hair, enjoying Ed's moment of discomfort too much.

Ed raked his hair back into place with a rough hand. 'I don't know what you're talking about.'

'Uh-huh. That's why you haven't been yourself lately.'

Ed couldn't deny it, so he said nothing. Jamie didn't need to know he was having trouble even building the motivation to get out of bed in the morning.

His little brother slapped him on the back. 'Oh, you've got it bad, haven't you?'

Losing Georgiana had been the wake-up call he'd needed to put things into perspective. To see that he was allowed to make a life for himself. He didn't love his family any less now, they simply didn't need *him* twenty-four hours a day. Arrangements had been made for help and he was always on the end of the phone if they really needed him. It was ironic that after making all this extra time for a relationship, he had no one to share it with. He'd waited too long to make the changes.

'See? It's this bad mood, the dejected look on your face, that I can't bear to put up with for another second. Sort yourself out.'

Jamie was right, he couldn't go on like this for ever. Georgiana had left him, and he was supposed to accept it. However painful.

The problem was, he didn't want to accept it.

He loved her.

Not that he'd told her so. He hadn't been clear about his feelings at all or honest with himself about what he wanted. His determination not to make room in his life for a new relationship meant that he'd let her slip away.

She hadn't known how important she was to him. He only had himself to blame for that.

And only he could make things right…

Georgiana's eyes were as heavy as the rest of her body and she struggled to open them.

'What's happening?' she slurred, her tongue stuck to the roof of her mouth because it was so dry.

'Do you need some water?'

There was a shuffling beside her as she tried to focus; she could see someone was at the side of her bed. 'Yes, please.'

'Just take enough to wet your lips for now,' instructed a familiar male voice.

Once she'd taken a sip and the effort of lifting her head proved impossible to sustain, she lay down again. It was difficult to think with the fog in her head but she eventually remembered where she was and what she was doing. 'I had an operation…'

'Yes, you did. Everything went well. You need to rest now.'

The voice comforted her. She didn't have anything to worry about. 'Sleep is good…' she mumbled and drifted happily back to oblivion.

When she awoke again, everything seemed

less fuzzy and she had a vague recollection of her last foray back to consciousness.

'Ed?' She was sure it was him she'd heard in her hospital room. Unless it was wishful thinking during her delirium. The room was empty of visitors when she glanced around, although there was a chair pulled up by her bed. There was no reason Ed, or anyone else, would be here. She hadn't told him about the operation and she'd asked her parents not to visit for the simple reason she saw no need to upset them. When she was recovered enough she'd go home and recover there with their support. It didn't mean she wasn't feeling sorry for herself now, groggy, in pain and alone. Missing her mother, father and Ed.

'You're awake.' As Ed walked into the room carrying what looked and smelled like vending-machine coffee she wondered if she was still half asleep.

'I thought I dreamed you,' she told him as he resumed his place by her bed.

'I was here. Waiting for you to come around. How are you feeling?'

'Tired and sore. How did you know I was here?' After their last encounter and ghosting him since, she'd never expected to see him again. Much less at her side when she came around post-op. Whatever his reason for being here, she was glad to see him. Ed was the boost she needed when she was in the doldrums.

He took a sip of his coffee and grimaced before setting it down on her nightstand. 'Will you kill her if I tell you your mother called me?'

'Yes.' She was even more curious now about the background to this visit if he'd spoken to her family.

His laugh was like medicine after these weeks spent without him. 'At least you're being honest. For once. I suspect you might have fibbed during our last conversation.'

She squirmed on the rustling hospital sheets, under his knowing gaze. 'What do you mean?'

He leaned closer to the bed. 'I hear you and my brother spoke too.'

'So? People are allowed to be concerned about you even if you don't listen to them.'

'Am I supposed to believe it's a coincidence that you're told you need further surgery and you decide being with me is the wrong thing to do?'

She wanted to say yes and front out the lie but couldn't. A change of subject would have to suffice. 'Why did you come, Ed?'

'In case you had some stupid idea in your

head that you didn't want me to think I *had* to take care of you. That you would steal time from my family if I wanted to be with you.'

'It's not an unreasonable assumption that you're the kind of man who'd volunteer for more charity work.'

He swore then, startling her with the ferocity of his expletive. 'What do I have to do to convince you I want to be with you? Faced with the prospect of losing you, I went back and took a good hard look at my life. I got help for my parents and talked to my brothers and sisters about sharing any responsibilities. All to show you I was serious about making a go of things with you and you wouldn't even take my calls.'

She was trying not to cry.

'I thought it was best for you.' For her too, when she'd been scared of becoming too reliant on him.

His smile gave her hope it wasn't too late to start again.

'I'm as much of a fan of people making decisions on my behalf as you are.'

'Point taken.'

He got up, squeezed onto the bed beside her and put his arm around her shoulders, pulling her close to his body; it was all the pain relief she needed.

'In case you were in any doubt, Princess, I'm mad about you. I wanted to be here when you woke up to make sure you were all right and to tell you I'll be here for as long as you want me. I love you.'

Georgiana tilted her face up to him and saw the truth in his words for herself. 'I love you too. Can we start over?'

She knew she could live without him, but the fact she didn't want to said everything about her feelings towards him.

'No. This means we can learn from our mistakes, be honest with each other and face the future together.' He kissed her on the lips, convincing her everything would be all right if he was there for her.

For once she was letting someone else control her narrative. After all, it was exactly the one she'd choose for herself.

EPILOGUE

Two years later

GEORGIANA WRAPPED HER arms around Ed's neck and let him carry her the short distance she needed to go. 'I hate this.'

'I know, but it's only temporary. It's to make things a little easier on you. Your body needs a rest and now so do I.' Ed set her gently into the wheelchair, with that mischievous grin of his firmly in place.

'Ha-ha. This is all your fault, you know.'

'I think it took two of us, sweetheart.' He dropped a kiss on her lips then moved behind the chair so he could push her. Georgiana had no choice but to sit back and let him. She was tired, sore and cranky but the extra weight she was carrying these days had taken its toll.

If she didn't want to stop working altogether this was the only way for her to get about the clinic. It had been a busy couple of years for them as a couple. Not only because the Love on a Limb charity had proved to be a resounding success and they were realising Ed's dream of hosting a national sports event, but Georgiana had also completed her training course and was helping with the hydrotherapy sessions at the clinic when she could. Her current condition hadn't been factored into their schedule but, as usual, they were facing it together.

'I suppose it'll all be worth it in the end.'

'Of course it will. It's everything we didn't know we wanted.' She could hear the smile in his voice and it went some way to alleviating her discomfort. Things were going to change again very soon but she had no doubt Ed was going to step up and be there for her as always.

She toyed with the chain around her neck where her engagement ring hung. Her fingers were too big to wear it any more but it meant as much as ever. As soon as things had settled down again and she was back to her old self they were going to set a date for the wedding. She couldn't wait to make it official and become Mrs Lawrence. He was living with them at the palace for now, since it was already adapted to suit her extra needs. Hopefully they'd have their own place soon.

'I can't wait until he's here.' Georgiana stroked her belly, willing little Freddie to come and meet them soon. She'd taken her folic acid religiously, had all the checks and their baby boy was as healthy as could be expected.

'I can't believe I'm going to be a father.' Even after nine months Ed couldn't seem to quite get his head around it.

'I never considered I'd ever be a mother but here we are, only days away from becoming parents, so we'd better get used to it.' She laughed. If she'd harboured any last niggles that she was somehow not a whole woman, finding out she was pregnant put paid to them.

They were going to be a family soon, no longer content with the solitary lives they'd once held so dear. Now being together was all that mattered.

* * * * *

If you enjoyed this story, check out these other great reads from Karin Baine

One Night with Her Italian Doc
Reunion with His Surgeon Princess
Healed by Their Unexpected Family
Their One-Night Christmas Gift

All available now!